Kinky Baby

Sugar Babies #1

Charity Parkerson

Copyright

KINKY BABY

Copyright © 2019 Charity Parkerson

Editor: BZ Hercules & Consultants

Cover Model: Martin C.

Photographer: Wander Aguiar

ISBN: 978-1-946099-49-5

Contents

Introduction

TRACE IS YOUNG, HOT, *and used to being the boss. Hunter isn't looking for any of that.*

When Trace moved from California to Colorado, it was only business. Raised by great businessmen, everything Trace touches turns to gold. At twenty, he's the youngest and most successful nightclub owner around. With an uncanny talent of always knowing the hottest trends, Trace has fattened his already bulging pockets. He's content with focusing on his career. Then he meets Hunter, and nothing feels right anymore.

Hunter's stress has stress. He doesn't have time for a young, hot, too-much-of-everything guy. In fact, Hunter's so busy drowning in debt and dealing with his son's issues, he doesn't have the energy for anyone. The last thing he needs is sexy, barely-classified-as-an-adult Trace taking over his life. But damn, Trace controls his every thought. Hunter doesn't know where to go with that. All Hunter knows is, he'd better find a way to let Trace in or lose him forever.

Kinky Baby is the first in a new series, Sugar Babies—a series of M/M romances centered on younger men who take care of their daddies. No matter which kink you love, hopefully, there will be a sugar baby for you.

Chapter One

THE ROADS WERE DEAD, considering it was a Saturday night. Trace wondered what most twenty-year-old people were out doing. Probably not picking up an employee because their club was short-handed a bartender and Saturday nights were too busy to be in that position. Technically, Lane McPherson wasn't an employee, although he would be on Trace's payroll tonight. Lane was only doing Trace a favor. Trace had moved to Aspen two weeks after his nineteenth birthday and opened Club Incubus with a loan from his father. Lane had been one of the first people Trace met. Since Lane bounced from bar to bar, working as bar back and never tied down to one place, he filled in whenever Trace needed him.

To most, a twenty-year-old running a nightclub might sound insane. Trace had been born with an independent streak a mile wide to two fathers who owned a bar. He'd been helping out in the industry for as long as he could remember. Being a businessman ran through his veins. Trace didn't know how to fail. He'd paid his father back in full six months after the club's opening and hadn't once touched his inheritance, as he'd promised his father when he'd set out on this path. Incubus was a bigger success than Trace or his father ever envisioned. If only people would show up to work, then Trace would be set.

Thankfully, Lane always came through. That meant a lot to Trace. If only he could find the dude's house. Trace slowed and checked the numbers on the closest mailbox. Fuck. He'd been looking on the wrong side of the street. Trace pulled into the nearest driveway and turned around. The subdivision was nice. Maybe upper middle class. Truthfully, Trace didn't pay much attention to house prices. He still lived in the same small cabin he'd rented shortly after moving to town. Trace might be a savvy businessman for his age, but there were still lots of things he didn't know if he wanted yet. His dad and stepdad lived in Southern California. Maybe he'd expand to that area or sell out and move home one day. Hell, he'd even considered hitting the East coast for a while.

The world was still his oyster, and nothing tied him down.

Trace spotted the number he'd been hunting. The medium-sized brick home looked well-maintained. The place was almost picturesque, surrounded by snow. Trace pointed his Range Rover down the driveway and followed it to the closed garage door.

Trace killed the engine and darted to the side door Lane had told him to use. It was too fucking cold for his blood. He loved looking at snow through a window, by a fire, while draped in blankets, and drinking the hottest of coffees. Otherwise, it could suck dick. He hated being cold. Thankfully, Lane opened the door before Trace's knuckles brushed the wood.

"Hey, man. Give me five minutes. Okay?"

Trace shrugged. "No worries. There's no rush." Trace's gaze slid toward a dark-haired guy standing in Lane's kitchen. He was busy cooking.

Lane followed Trace's stare. He motioned the man's way. "Oh, yeah. This is my dad. Dad, this is Trace. He's the guy I'm always telling you about." Lane walked away, leaving them alone without a second glance.

The guy met Trace's stare. His eyes were gorgeous. They were hazel, which wasn't that unique, but they had sexy fine lines in the corners that deepened when he smiled. He swiped his hand on his jeans before holding it out for Trace to shake. "Hey, Trace. You can call me Hunter, being as how I'm not your dad," he tacked on with a laugh and an adorable little wink.

It was like Hunter triggered something inside Trace, flipping his flirt button to the on position. Trace didn't release his hand. "We've just met. Give me five minutes. You might decide you'd enjoy having me call you Daddy." A sexy rumble of laughter filled the space between them. Trace took a breath. Damn. The guy was gorgeous. Trace couldn't stop. "Don't worry. I'm not searching for anyone to take care of me. Not financially anyhow. There are other needs, though."

Hunter retrieved his hand. "Are you always on like this?"

"Only when I spot someone worthwhile," Trace answered honestly. "Otherwise, I'm pretty focused on my business. What are you cooking? It smells good. Or is that you?"

Hunter shook his head, fighting a smile. Goddamn it was sexy. Trace spotted a hint of dimple. "It's taco soup. Are you hungry? I could pack you some to go."

"I'm famished, but no. By the time I get a chance to eat, it'll be cold. But thank you. If I had time, I would definitely take you up on that. I'm intrigued." Trace let the words hang in the air just long enough to ensure Hunter wondered if he meant the soup or Hunter had his interest. Hunter watched him. He looked as if he held his breath. "I've never had taco soup," he added, putting Hunter out of his misery. Hunter glanced away. Trace hid a smile. "Or a friend's dad." Hunter's lips twisted, fighting a smile. Trace's brain fired on all cylinders. He loved making other people smile.

"Okay. I'm ready," Lane said, appearing from the mouth of the hallway. "Thanks for picking me up. Until I can afford some new tires, my car isn't going any-where in the snow."

Trace cast a longing glance Hunter's way. His white V-neck t-shirt clung to his solid chest. A hint of chest hair peeked out from the top. There wasn't anything Trace could pinpoint that snagged his attention, but damn. He was interested. "It's no problem. I'm glad I came by. Otherwise, I think I would've missed out."

"Okay," Lane said, dragging the word out in his obvious confusion.

Trace still didn't tear his gaze away from Hunter's hazel stare. "You should join us."

An uncomfortable-sounding chuckle escaped Hunter. "No. I don't think so. I'm a bit old for that scene."

The twitching of Trace's lips was out of his control. Hunter wasn't old. Trace didn't think the guy would appreciate it if he laughed at the ridiculousness of his statement. Instead, Trace reached inside his jacket to the inner pocket and pulled out a card. He set it on the bar separating the kitchen from the dining area. "Here's the address. In case you change your mind. A guy named Walker mans the door. Tell him I asked you to come. He'll let you in for free. I'll tell him to keep an eye out for you."

"He'll be wasting his time." Hunter didn't sound like he was trying to be rude. He was just attempting to keep Trace in his place as Lane's friend.

But Trace had confidence on his side. "Hope is never a waste of time."

To Trace's surprise, a hint of sadness passed over Hunter's features. "Well, now that's not true in the least."

Something shifted in Trace's chest. He'd never been the type who could stand suffering. His dad claimed it was because he had a soul of gold. Trace didn't believe that. He just thought if a person had happiness to spare, they should.

"I'd make it worthwhile for you to be there."

Hunter's gaze sharpened, as if he really looked at Trace for the first time at Trace's serious tone. His mouth lifted in one corner, making Trace wish for his thoughts. "I'll think about it."

Trace winked, taking what he could get. He followed Lane out the door with a final wave. They made it halfway to the club before Lane mentioned the encounter. "That was nice of you to invite my dad. He doesn't really do anything but work and stress about money since Mom died."

Trace kept his gaze locked on the road. "He seems awful young to be your dad."

When Lane responded, he sounded distracted as he played on his phone. "That's because he's not my biological father. I was four when he started dating my mom. Mom was seven years older than him. He adopted me after they married. He's the only dad I've ever known. Now it's just the two of us."

That was sad and eerily familiar. Trace's father had died almost four years earlier. He'd been certain his other dad would never recover. Now he was remarried to an awesome guy. Trace hated the thought of Hunter staying home all alone. "How is it I've known you for over a year and this is the first time I'm meeting him?"

Lane glanced over and snorted. "You never leave your club for any reason other than to go home or back to Cali."

Trace couldn't argue with that. "I'll give you that much."

"It's not like I've met your family either."

That was also true. He needed to change the subject before he showed how interested he truly was in Lane's too sexy father. "Thanks for helping me out tonight."

Out of the corner of his eye, he saw Lane shrug. "It's no big deal. I need the money. Plus, like I said when you called, you're rescuing me from the house. Maybe I'll get enough tips tonight to get new tires."

"I'll buy your tires," Trace offered on impulse. "You always come through for me when I'm shorthanded."

"You don't have to do that. I'm not trying to take advantage of our friendship."

Trace shrugged. "I can afford it. Don't worry over it. It's hard enough running this club with another year left before I can even buy the liquor for the place. It matters a lot that you're always willing to help when everyone else backs out. I still think you should come work for me full-time."

"You don't want that." Lane sounded sad. Trace glanced over, but he couldn't see Lane's expression in the dark. "Never mix business with friendship, right?" he said, brightening.

"Hmmm," Trace hummed noncommittally. People always said that, and in a way, they were right, except when they were wrong. In Trace's limited experience, he had better luck with people he considered friends. It was when people didn't like him that they didn't show up for their shifts, screwing Trace on nights he was already shorthanded, but whatever. He liked Lane. Trace would make sure he got new tires. It was the least he could do.

Trace spent the night watching for Hunter. As expected, he didn't show. There'd been a small spark of hope Hunter would shock him, but no. Trace got tired of the club scene sometimes, but this was his job. Like with any job, there were times when he wanted a night off. Since he didn't have that luxury right now, he'd really hoped Hunter would come and distract him. Instead, it was the same guys who always hit on Trace. No amount of disinterest on his part ever dissuaded them. The club cleared out early due to worsening weather conditions. Trace decided to close early. Still, he found himself watching for Hunter with no reasonable explanation.

"Why do you keep looking at the door? Are you expecting someone?"

Trace tore his gaze away from the door and focused on Walker. "I was, but he didn't show. It's too late now, but I guess I've trained myself to keep looking." He concentrated on pulling the plastic off a sucker and popping it in his mouth, hoping to hide his disappointment.

"I'm glad to hear you're making new friends," Walker said, sounding distracted. "Anyone at all is better than that ass you keep showing up with."

That caught Trace's attention. "Who? Lane?"

Walker caught his eye and held his stare. His dark expression screamed Trace was a fool. "Yes, Lane."

"What's wrong with Lane?"

Walker rolled his eyes and went back to flipping through the receipts. "What's he doing right now?"

Trace looked toward the bar. Lane was talking to a server, being as animated as possible. His blond hair stood in every direction. A smile pulled at the corners of Trace's mouth. He liked Lane. The guy was almost always on, brightening every room. Trace half expected Lane to bust out some Kungfu moves. In some ways, he reminded Trace of himself. "He's just a clown. He likes to make people laugh."

An ugly-sounding snort escaped Walker. Trace looked closer at him. It wasn't like Walker to dislike anyone. It was obvious Lane was on that short list. "He's not a clown," Walker argued while focused on his job. "He's an addict. That's not entertaining others. He's high as fuck."

That too, but he was off the clock and just hanging out until Trace could take him home. "You probably described half the people who came tonight. What's different about Lane?"

Walker's huge shoulder lifted in a half shrug, but he didn't say more. Lane appeared at Trace's side. He slid across the arm of the loveseat and landed in Trace's lap. "Take me home, baby," he said, wrapping his arms around Trace's neck.

Trace laughed while Lane placed a loud, wet kiss on his cheek. "You're the tenth person to ask. What makes you special?"

"I can't drive, and I put out." Lane cuddled against Trace's chest, sounding ready to pass out.

"Okay, angel. Let's go. I'm not carrying your ass out." He glanced Walker's way. "Are you cool to close up? Seriously, I can't carry his ass out."

"Yeah. You'd better go then." Walker did not sound happy. Great. He'd have to do something special for the guy—like a hefty bonus.

Trace moved to stand. Lane was already out. "Fuck." He liked Lane—in spite of all his faults— but this was too much. He looked to Walker for help.

Walker growled as he stood. "Tell me again why you like this idiot." Walker grumbled each word as he tossed Lane over his shoulder and headed for the door.

"I'll make this up to you," Trace said, hoping to diffuse the situation as he scrambled after Walker. He couldn't lose his manager. The man kept him in business.

At the door, Walker paused, waiting for Trace to open it for him. Their gazes met. Walker looked darker than Trace had ever seen him. "You're a good person, Trace. One of these days, that golden soul of yours is going to cost you everything if you keep giving it all away to people like this."

Despite Walker's warning, a bright smile lit Trace's face. "You sound like my dad."

"Someone has to," Walker muttered as he headed outside. Trace's humor wasn't affected. He knew Walker cared about him, but Trace had plenty love to go around. He understood what it was like to be lonely, and he had no intention of abandoning anyone.

Chapter Two

FOR THE HUNDREDTH TIME since Trace left, Hunter found himself staring into space and shaking his head. There was no way that child had been flirting with him. Hunter was old. There was no way that boy was out of his teens. He was—at the very most—twenty. Hunter shook his head. There was no way. An image of Trace's light blue eyes, flashing with interest, floated through Hunter's head again. Heat rushed to his face. Damn. He missed being young and sexy. Once upon a time, he'd been just as confident as Trace, sure of his ability to have any-one he set his sights on. Surely Trace hadn't been flirting with him.

With another shake of his head, Hunter stood and wandered through the house. He'd worked so hard for so many years to have this place. When Lacy and he had bought this house, only months after they'd married, they'd planned to grow old here. Fifteen years later, cancer had stolen her away and now Hunter was one missed payment away from foreclosure. Hunter rubbed his chest. The place felt empty tonight. He found himself standing outside Lane's closed bedroom door. His fingers closed around the knob. Lane had been four years old when Hunter started dating Lacy. On his tenth birthday, they'd sur-prised Lane with adoption papers. He'd legally become the dad he'd always been in his heart. It was a job he'd failed at more epically than he'd ever bombed at anything in his life. Hunter let his fingers slip away from the doorknob. He was better off not knowing what was inside.

Hunter stared at his bare feet as he padded down the hall. He'd installed these hardwood floors. Hunter snorted. He'd been sure of his ability to do anything back then. Now he couldn't even fathom a young, hot, and overly confident mess flirting with him. Hunter released a loud sigh just to fill the silence. He'd taken a shower and pulled on pajama pants an hour earlier, determined to go to bed. The house was too quiet. He couldn't relax. The moment Hunter stepped inside the kitchen, he spotted Trace's card still sitting on the counter. With no real plan in mind, Hunter picked up the card. A smile tugged at the corners of his mouth. The paper was thick and felt expensive. An image of a demon with Club Incubus printed over it filled the front. Hunter flipped it over. Trace's number stared up at him. It was obvious this was a personal card. One given to clients... or hookups. There wasn't an address and the number looked like it belonged to a cell-phone. Hunter chewed his bottom lip to stop another smile. Hunger hit without warning. There was so much about living that Hunter missed. He dropped the card before temptation made him weak. He needed pie. That was all. He was not lusting after some man-child who had a stack of cards ready to hand out to anyone and everyone who caught his eye.

Hunter opened the fridge and stared at the contents. Another image of Trace took control of Hunter's brain. He was so baby-faced, except for those lips.

They were full and meant for sin. Hunter tugged open the freezer and let the cold air wash over him, hoping to cool his overheated skin. Goddamn it. He was interested. A loud snort escaped Hunter. He'd be a fool not to be intrigued. It wasn't every day an offer like Trace came around after forty. He wouldn't call, but he was flattered.

The back door flew open. Lane spilled in with Trace holding him up, keeping him from falling onto the floor.

"Where's his room?" Trace asked, sounding every bit as annoyed as he should.

Hunter waved toward the hall. "This way." He led Trace down the hall while swallowing the hurt and anger—the way he always did. Hunter knew he should probably offer to take over. Lane wasn't Trace's problem. He was too enraged. If it was left to him, Trace could drop Lane where they stood. It was not like Lane would feel it until the morning. Instead, he calmly opened Lane's bedroom door and stood by as Trace dumped Lane in bed. Trace turned. Their gazes met. The tightness in Hunter's chest eased.

"I'm sorry." Hunter couldn't stop the apology. Even he didn't know exactly what he was sorry about. Too many things, really.

Trace's mouth lifted in one corner. "It's not a big deal."

Yes. It was. "Would you like some coffee?"

Trace's gaze dropped to Hunter's bare chest before lifting to meet Hunter's stare again. "It's two a.m."

"Is it really?"

"Yes," Lane croaked out behind Trace, sounding annoyed. "Turn out the light."

The tightness in Hunter's chest was back. He left the light on as he walked away. Trace closed the door with an audible snap as he left Lane's room without turning off the light. The move made Hunter smile. It seemed he wasn't the only one irritated by Lane's bullshit.

"You didn't show tonight. Last night. Whatever," Trace said behind him.

"I knew if I waited long enough, the party would come to me." Hunter couldn't have stopped the bitterness in his voice if he tried. "It always does," he muttered under his breath.

Trace didn't respond. He held his silence for so long, Hunter gave in the moment he stood at the kitchen counter. Hunter found himself staring at Trace, trying to decipher his expression. He looked understanding.

"He's young."

A bark of laughter escaped him at Trace's observation. "So are you." Hunter felt moved to point out the obvious.

Trace's smile was way too sexy for Hunter's comfort. "Yes. I'm young. But according to my dad, the one who's passed, not the one who's still living, I've always been an old soul. They owned a popular bar in California when I was a kid, so I was raised around the scene. I've seen time and time again what diving headlong into the partying lifestyle does to people. That's not for me."

"Yet you own a nightclub," Hunter said, pointing out the obvious.

Trace's smile grew. "I didn't say I was above profiting from everyone else's choices."

Despite his mood over the Lane situation, Hunter found himself smiling. There was something about Trace. It was like he was so full of life and vitality that he energized Hunter.

Trace's smile slipped away. His expression turned heated. "You're incredibly sexy."

God help him. Lust sideswiped him—hard. A blush exploded through his face. Hunter wished he wore a shirt. He felt exposed beneath Trace's stare.

"I make you uncomfortable."

Damn. Hunter wished he could deny it. "You're very young," Hunter said, scrambling to stand on the opposite side of the counter.

Trace set his keys on the counter and focused on Hunter. "Is that really why I make you so uneasy?" Trace paused for a heartbeat as if only stopping to confirm his belief Hunter wouldn't answer before continuing. "Or maybe it's not discomfort but something else, like you're restless because you want me too."

Hunter couldn't stop smiling. Trace was so ridiculously over-confident. "You're easily the cockiest person I've ever met."

"I'm not hearing a denial."

Hunter chuckled. "You're ridiculous."

Trace turned serious in an instant, making Hunter's breath catch. He suddenly wondered which version of Trace was the real one—the too-cocky flirt or this? "You're smiling. My job is complete. I'll leave you to enjoy the rest of your night." He pushed away from the counter.

Hunter's throat swelled. In an instant, he wanted to beg Trace not to take the happiness away. As always, when it came time to save himself, Hunter stayed silent.

Trace pointed at Hunter as he headed for the door. "Don't lose my number. I expect you to text me by tomorrow."

Hunter shook his head. Trace's confidence was hard to resist. "Be careful going home. I'm sure the roads are getting worse by the minute."

Somehow Trace managed to brighten even more. "And to think you didn't want me calling you Daddy."

Before Hunter could roll his eyes, Trace turned and slipped out the door. Hunter bit his lip, hiding his smile from his conscience. Damn. Trace was so young, and... wow. Hunter fought the urge to cover his face. This whole thing was ridiculous. With a sigh, he pushed away from the bar that had kept him safe from making an ass of himself. His gaze landed on the card Trace left behind. Trace's keys sat next to it.

"Fuck." Hunter snatched up the set and headed for the door. He threw it open. "You forgot—"

"I forgot—"

They ran into each other chest to chest and froze. Neither of them made any move to step away as they blocked the same doorway. To his horror, Hunter was hard enough to bend steel with the too-cocky Trace pressed fully against him.

One of Trace's eyebrows rose. Just one. There was a challenge in that. "Would you like to talk about the erection between us?"

Hunter shook his head. "I don't know what you're talking about." Was it a dumbass thing to say? Yes. Was he sticking by it? Also, yes.

"All right then." Trace snagged his keys and headed for his car. Hunter's eyes refused to give up the treat of watching Trace's every move. He walked with so much self-assurance. Goddamn. Trace was younger than Hunter's son, for fuck's sakc. What sort of old pervert was he? "You should probably stop staring at my ass if you're pretending you're not interested," Trace called over his shoulder.

"I never said I wasn't interested," Hunter muttered under his breath.

Trace turned and closed the distance between them so fast, Hunter couldn't react. He simply found himself staring into eyes so blue, they should be outlawed. His hands itched to touch Trace's dark blond hair. "What was that? I didn't quite understand you from way over there."

"I don't date men anymore." God help him. He couldn't stop his mouth from saying stupid shit.

Trace smirked. Hunter couldn't blame him. Even to his ears, he sounded like an idiot. "That's too bad. You'll probably hate this, then." That was all the warning Hunter got before Trace hauled him forward and claimed his mouth. He tasted like cherry candy. Goddamn. Hunter's knees weakened. This was wrong. So fucking wrong. Trace was a kid compared to him and a guy. Hunter had sworn men off years before Lacy. Goddamn. He couldn't stop. Hunter didn't touch Trace in any way, but he kissed Trace back. He couldn't pretend he didn't chase after every drop of candy coating the guy's tongue.

"Come to my car with me," Trace cajoled between kisses. "I can do things you've only fantasized about to that erection that doesn't exist."

Hunter pulled away. This was nuts. He couldn't do this. "I'm probably a good twenty-five years older than you. There's nothing you can show me I haven't seen. You should go. This shouldn't have happened."

Trace winked. "You're adorable when you lie to yourself. See you around."

Hunter nearly melted to the floor as Trace walked away. He was fucking perfect. Hunter fought a whimper. Of all the things he'd ever denied himself, a night with Trace probably hit in the top three. Hunter didn't give up the show of Trace's ass walking away. For a moment, he almost caved. He wondered which he would regret more—a night with Trace or missing a night with Trace. While fighting back his longing, Hunter turned away and froze. Lane stood watching him, looking strangely sober for someone who'd forced Trace to help him to bed only minutes earlier.

"Did that just happen?"

While keeping his expression carefully blank, Hunter did the only thing he could. He lied. "I don't know what you mean."

Lane pointed toward the open door behind Hunter and then to Hunter. His gaze swung between the two. Hunter had never seen his son look more stunned. "That. You. Trace. He kissed you. You let him. Offers were made. I mean, I'm high, but I've never been *that* high."

"It's sad that I'm so used to my son being fucked up that not only does the news bounce right off me, you no longer have an ounce of shame saying it out loud." Was he dodging by turning the conversation to Lane's faults? Possibly. Hunter gave no fucks.

Lane swiped his hand through the air. "Never mind that. This is a good thing," Lane said, looking way too happy. "He's rich. Like swimming in money. If you're going gay, now's the time."

"Going gay," Hunter scoffed. "That's not a thing. People are born one way or the other or something in between, but people don't go gay. That's..." He didn't actually know what that was, but he didn't think it was a thing.

"But you let him kiss you."

Hunter decided to brazen it out. He shrugged. "So? It happened. He kissed me. I wasn't going to shove a kid down the garage stairs to get away from him. He made a move. I wasn't interested. End of story."

"But you have to be interested," Lane said, sounding desperate. "I need him to invest in my business. What'll it hurt for you to go on one date?"

"Have you seen me date anyone since your mom passed?" Even Hunter heard the dryness in his tone. They weren't having this conversation.

Lane shrugged. "I don't do dick either, but you can bet your ass if Trace Thomson—a man worth literally millions—offered to get me off, I'd be all over it."

"I didn't say I don't do dick. It so happens I dated several men before I fell in love with your mom," Hunter muttered more to himself than Lane, since Lane wasn't listening.

"Dad, you can't afford to be squeamish."

Hunter scrubbed his hands over his face. "I'm not squeamish. There's nothing wrong with him."

"That's the spirit," Lane said, cutting in and refusing to let it go. "You're about to lose this house. I need him to back my dispensary. Trace is loaded and obviously interested in you. It's time to take one for the team. I'd do it if he was after me."

"We're not discussing this," Hunter said, putting his foot down. "I'm going to bed."

"Dad."

"No," Hunter said, cutting Lane off before he pissed Hunter off for real. "Goodnight." At the last second, Hunter snagged Trace's business card off the counter as he passed. His irritation carried him all the way to his bedroom. Once the door closed behind him, Hunter deflated. He didn't understand why everything always had to be so hard. Some days, it felt like Hunter had nothing left of himself. When he'd married Lacy, Hunter had become her husband and Lane's dad. Everything he'd been before then disappeared. Losing his individual identity hadn't mattered until she was gone. Now, nothing ever felt right. Hunter looked down at the card in his hand. What if he did something completely out of the norm? Maybe he was still hiding inside himself somewhere. He could text Trace. If no one knew, then no one would know. To Hunter's still slightly lust-filled brain, his thoughts made complete sense. Trace was extremely young, but he was legal. It wasn't like Trace had any real interest in Hunter beyond the physical. If Hunter didn't tell anyone, it could be something for him alone. A step toward reclaiming himself.

Hunter's gaze landed on his phone by the bed. He inched forward. One text. He would send one text, and then if Trace didn't respond, Hunter would pretend tonight never happened. Hunter grabbed his phone before he changed his mind. After programming Trace as a new contact, Hunter sent Trace a quick message.

Hunter: *It's Hunter. Don't read this while driving. This is my number.*

There. No big deal. He'd thrown the ball into Trace's court. It was up to Trace to decide now. Hunter set the phone aside and took several deep breaths. Hoping to make himself believe he didn't care if Trace texted back, Hunter went through the motions of getting ready for bed. He went through his nightly routine of brushing his teeth, turning out the lights and stripping down to his underwear. The second he slipped beneath the sheets, his phone vibrated, sounding loud as hell in the silence. While chewing his bottom lip, Hunter opened the text.

Trace: *I'm home. The roads aren't that bad. So... phone sex?*

A smile exploded across Hunter's face along with a blush. He couldn't pretend the heat burning his face was anything else.

Hunter: *I'm glad you made it home safely. It doesn't seem like it took you long. Where is home?*

Yeah, he realized he'd dodged the whole phone sex thing, but he felt stupid enough as things were.

Trace: *Technically, my real home is in California, but I'm renting a small cabin off Waverly. You're avoiding my question.*

Hunter: *Technically? Does that mean you think of Colorado as temporary?*

The phone rang in Hunter's hand, startling him. He took a deep breath and answered. "Hello?"

"Why are you dodging?"

Hunter rolled onto his back and stared at the dark ceiling. Even Trace's voice was sexy. Just hearing Trace speak filled the air with new life. Hunter wondered what it must be like to have such an electrifying personality. "I'm not dodging as much as I'm trying to get to know you better."

"Okay," Trace said, sounding completely fine with Hunter's decision, ratcheting up Hunter's interest and respect. Something brushed across the phone—like Trace was multitasking. "To answer your last text, I'm not sure. I like it here. It's beautiful and I've made some great friends, but California is equally gorgeous, and my family is there. Some days, I think I'll stay put. Other days, I wonder if I should go home. Then there are days when I plan my next move someplace completely different. In the end, I do nothing because I don't know what I want."

That was fair. Hunter was forty-two, and he still didn't know what he wanted either. Curiosity won. "How old are you anyhow?"

"Twenty."

Hunter's brain froze. He wasn't twenty-five years older than Trace as he'd obnoxiously claimed earlier, but fuck. It was a near thing.

"Did I break you?" Trace asked with a sexy-sounding chuckle.

Hunter cleared his throat. "No. I'm just wrapping my head around a twenty-year-old running a nightclub."

"Why is my age always the first thing someone comments on when it comes to my job?" Trace said the words as if they were more for himself than Hunter. "It's a business I understand," Trace said louder, bringing the conversation back to Hunter. "As I said earlier, my parents owned a popular bar. I learned at the feet of the best. Age has nothing to do with it."

"I only brought up your age because you're not old enough to buy liquor, so a nightclub seemed an odd choice."

When Trace responded, he sounded mollified. "Ah, but my parents are Scottish. Their ideas about the legal drinking age are somewhat different."

Hunter marveled over Trace's sudden Scottish accent. It was perfect—like he was the bilingual version of accents. "Does that mean you were born in Scotland?"

"No," Trace said. Something else brushed across the phone—like he was still doing something else while talking to Hunter. "But I was homeschooled. So, for a long time, I had the same accent as my parents, since it was all that I heard. I didn't start losing the brogue until I was in my late teens."

Being homeschooled explained a lot. Trace hadn't spent time around other kids and it showed. He'd probably always been an adult. The more Trace spoke, the more Hunter relaxed. The age gap between them didn't seem as wide.

"What about you, sexy? What do you do?"

Hunter smiled at the easy way Trace complimented him. Gah. He liked him. This shouldn't be happening. Yet Hunter couldn't stop. "I'm an architect."

"Interesting. Tell me more."

Hunter laughed. Trace really sounded interested, and it was sweet. "Really, it's not. I used to think it was fascinating to watch something I designed become reality." Hunter shrugged without thought. "Now it's just a job, I guess."

"You have a nice home. There's no such thing as just a job if it's keeping a roof over your head."

Except it wasn't and having the truth of things slap him in the face again nearly took his breath. "Actually, the house is mostly thanks to my wife, Lacy. She was a radiologist. Now I'm not doing so great at keeping up with the payments. Wow," Hunter said, trying to lighten the tone. "I didn't mean to get all serious on you. Didn't you say something about phone sex?" Because anything at all was better than reality, even humiliating himself with a younger man.

Silence met Hunter's question, doubling his discomfort. He opened his mouth to tell Trace goodbye. Trace spoke, killing the words in Hunter's throat. "My dad died when I was sixteen, completely leveling my other dad's life. It's okay if you don't feel like you're ready to be talking to me."

Like that, there was nothing Hunter wanted more than to talk to Trace. He didn't hesitate to admit it. "Honestly? I don't know why, but there's nothing I'd rather be doing. Why do you taste like cherries?" Hunter smiled into the dark as he asked the question. The mortification over the situation had slipped away at some point. Now Hunter just felt interested.

A sexy hum came through the line. "You went straight for the hard-hitting question. I'm addicted to these cherry suckers they sell at the gas station across from my club. Well, honestly, you can probably buy them other places too, but that's the only place I've seen them. I swear they're lacing them with something, because I can't stop. Or maybe I just have an oral fixation."

Hunter went hard. There was no building of arousal. One second, he was focused on the cadence of Trace's voice. The next, his hand slid south to adjust his erection. Still, he found himself laughing at Trace's inability to behave.

"How did you get like this? You say you were homeschooled, and I picture this sweet, sheltered child. Instead, you're incorrigible."

"I like your laugh," Trace said instead of answering. Hunter almost sighed. Trace continued, saving Hunter from himself. "I'm not sure how to answer this one without sounding like a freak." Trace's laughter sounded uncomfortable, making Hunter's curiosity skyrocket. "Um, so my dad used to be one of the most requested masters at a BDSM club, until he met my stepdad. He wasn't exactly good at hiding his gear and whatnot, and I was always home alone with his stuff and bored. I'm a child of kink. A kinky baby, if you will. I like a lot of you know..."

"Damn." Hunter couldn't have stopped the arousal-filled curse if he tried. The instant image Trace's confession painted in Hunter's perverted brain of Trace experimenting with his body was shameful on too many levels to count.

"You sound so turned on right now. That makes me wish I hadn't given up so easily earlier."

"It wouldn't have mattered," Hunter admitted. "I turned around to find Lane watching us, so that would've killed any progress you made."

"Oops."

Hunter chuckled at Trace's unapologetic tone. "Yeah. Awkward."

"I can't imagine Lane caring," Trace said, sounding thoughtful. "He praised me for inviting you out in the first place. I think he wants you to be happy."

Right now, Hunter didn't want to talk about Lane. He wanted to know exactly how Trace sounded when turned on.

Hunter had given in to temptation and texted Trace to step out of his comfort zone. He still wanted that. "What about you? What do you want?"

"I definitely want you to be happy."

Trace's tone was getting closer to what Hunter needed. "We're talking about you. Right now, in this moment, what's your heart's biggest desire?"

"In this moment?" Trace hummed, as if thinking things over. "If I could have anything, you would've come to the car with me earlier."

Hunter's cheeks ached from smiling. "That brings up a different question. Why the car? Why didn't you ask me to take you to bed?"

Trace's voice lowered, turning sultry. "We wouldn't have been alone inside. I don't want you stifling any sounds, worrying who'd hear."

"You saw where Lane's room is. Mine is on the opposite side of the house. We can't hear anything the other does when we're in our rooms."

"Does that mean I can sneak in your window and play?"

"Or you could come through the door," Hunter said, laughing.

"That sounded a lot like a yes on the getting to play with you."

Hunter covered his eyes, hiding his embarrassment, even though no one could see. "Damn. It really did, didn't it?"

Trace chuckled. "You're adorable. I swear I can hear your blush."

"Why aren't you blushing?" Hunter said louder than intended in his horror.

"Things should definitely be the other way around here. I should be the one shamelessly seducing you while you blush in horror."

"Seduce me then."

Goddamn it. Hunter kept finding himself cornered with no way out. He liked it. "Do I need to, or can I just say, 'take off your pants'?"

"Okay."

"Okay, what?"

"My pants are off," Trace said as if it was a done deal.

"Really?"

"Yep," Trace said, making the p pop. "I've been ready to go since you scurried around that bar in your kitchen to get away from me.

"I wasn't—" Fuck it. Yeah, he was. Hunter couldn't even lie. Not to mention, arguing wasted precious time. "That kiss, though," he said instead.

"Agreed."

Hunter didn't know how Trace made one word sound so damn sexy, but Hunter was on fire. "I haven't kissed anyone in a long time," Hunter admitted.

"When we're done here, I'll text you my address. You can find me anytime you want more. I'm especially fond of kissing. Oral fixation, remember?"

Wow. Hunter really wanted to know what else Trace liked doing with his mouth. "As if I could forget. If your pants are gone, what else are you wearing?"

"Nothing." Trace made the admission so easily. "I stripped when I came through the door. My clothes always smell like liquor when I leave the club. It's disgusting. Then you mentioned phone sex, and I was hopeful. What about you?"

So he'd be telling the truth, Hunter shimmied out of his underwear before answering. "I'm nude too."

"I could be there in twenty minutes."

"I'm not sure I can wait that long," Hunter admitted. He was beyond feeling ashamed. The way pre-cum dripped on his stomach was telling. Not only did he not have the patience to wait for Trace to drive back, he was scared to cool off and think. Right now, his brain was functioning only enough to keep his dick hard and his mouth moving.

"Fair enough. Tomorrow night?"

Hunter's bravery wavered. "I'm not sure."

"Tomorrow, Hunter. Tell me you'll be ready to go at eight and I'll tell you what I'm doing right now."

"I'll be ready." There was no way Hunter would miss hearing what Trace was doing.

"Good. So, I have this toy. It slips just over my crown and vibrates."

"Damn." Hunter palmed his cock.

A heat-inducing deep breath came through the line. "I don't know what it is about nothing else touching my dick anywhere else while this thing vibrates on the head, but it's mind-blowing. That's something I keep in mind while sucking dick."

Hunter took a deep breath. He couldn't stop stroking himself. He wanted to be in Trace's mouth.

"I have to be honest, Hunter. Sucking dick is one of my favorite things. Would you let me if I was there?"

"Fuck, I'm ready to beg you now. If you were here, I think I'd let you do and have whatever you want."

"You're what I want. I know you were married to a woman for a long time, but I'm still really hoping you'll let me fuck you."

A shiver ran through Hunter. He missed sex. All of it.

"Can I fuck you, Hunter?"

"Yes." Goddamn. That was his voice, needy and breathless. "I want you."

"I know you're turned on right now, but I expect you to stand by your word. It doesn't have to be tomorrow night. I can wait until you're ready, but you are seeing me tomorrow night. Now ride your fingers and pretend it's me."

Damn. It wasn't right for this twenty-year-old boy to make him feel so much, want so much, but Hunter wasn't turning him away. Hunter closed his eyes and jacked off. Trace's kiss filled his mind.

"Am I in your head yet?"

Hunter had no idea how Trace still sounded so calm and managed to talk. "Yes." Because fuck him, Trace was in his head.

"Damn," Trace cursed, sounding sexier than anyone had the right. "I can't wait to taste you. I wish you would've let me stay. You might not think I have anything to show you, but I might've surprised you."

He didn't need to tell Hunter. A hairs-breadth from orgasm, Hunter understood Trace probably did have a trick or two he hadn't seen. He also wished he hadn't been such a chicken shit and let Trace stay. He swore he could already feel Trace's hot mouth wrapped around his cock.

"Come for me, Hunter. Don't hold back."

A loud pant escaped Hunter. His strokes quickened. Trace was there with him in his mind. His sexy voice caressed Hunter's ear. Hunter's breath froze in his lungs. Everything went still. The pressure beating at his crown exploded. Cum coated his stomach. Moans vibrated from his throat. Hunter struggled for air as the sticky mess covering his skin cooled.

"Goddamn. That was hot. I can't wait to see it firsthand."

A soft, tired-sounding chuckle escaped Hunter. "I don't think you enjoyed this as much I did. You sound completely unaffected."

"You have no idea how blown away I am. I only wish I was there. You have sexy dimples. I'm feeling the loss of seeing them right now."

Hunter blinked at the ceiling while still trying to catch his breath. Trace was... nice. He was also naughty, but the nice part surprised Hunter more than he realized before now. Under any other circumstances, Hunter might've been slightly embarrassed right now. Instead, Trace simply made Hunter wish he hadn't sent him away—like it was completely natural for their night to end together. In that moment, it seemed odd as hell they'd just met.

"I don't know what to think." Hunter had no idea why he'd admitted that out loud. Something about Trace was really fucking with him.

"Don't. You strike me as the type who overdoes it. I can't wait to see you again."

Hunter swallowed. He was oddly overwhelmed. "Same."

"Get some sleep."

He wasn't sure he could. As Trace had claimed, Hunter usually did overthink things. He had a bad feeling he'd be thinking about Trace all night. "Okay."

"Tomorrow. Eight o'clock."

Hunter nodded like Trace could see him. "I'll be ready."

"Good. Sweet dreams, sexy."

"You too." Even though Hunter knew he needed to move and clean up his mess, he kept staring at the ceiling. For the life of him, he couldn't figure out what happened to his life in a span of just a few hours. He sort of felt like he'd been hit by a fast-moving train. Tomorrow, he would act his age. No doubt, Trace would move along quickly. It was for the best if he did. Still, no matter how hard Hunter tried, he couldn't regret anything. He'd been trapped for so long under the weight of his problems, this was the first time he'd breathed in forever. It was possible the whole encounter with Trace had been a fluke. The boy might not show tomorrow. An odd pang hit Hunter's chest. Hunter refused to listen to the tiny voice of hope in the back of his mind that whispered he'd met someone nice. With a snort, Hunter rolled from the bed. He'd always been a bit of a hopeless romantic. Trace would move along in no time. For now, Hunter would enjoy Trace as much as he could. No regrets.

<hr>

Trace spent a minute staring at the Club Incubus sign, trying to get his body under control. He'd hired a local artist to design the logo. It had turned out pretty badass in Trace's opinion. Truly, he loved this place. No one understood how hard he'd worked. Hunter thought he was too young. Even though Trace knew it, he thought he could overcome that opinion like he had everything else. A smile touched Trace's lips. He didn't think Hunter had worried too much about Trace's age while coming to the fantasy of him. Trace hated that he hadn't seen it in real life. He would eventually. Trace felt it in his gut.

With a sigh, he pushed open his car door and headed for the club. The place was mostly dark now. Only the hint of light shone through the glass front door. As much as he wished he'd actually been home to join Hunter in their phone sex session, the workaholic in him felt guilty as hell for leaving Walker alone to handle everything. He also hadn't expected Hunter's text. There'd been no way Trace would miss out on chatting with the guy. Hot was hot, and Trace recognized a good shot when he saw one.

Walker's chin jerked up from where he'd been staring at the same stack of receipts as when Trace left him earlier. A line formed between his gorgeous brown eyes. "Hey. I thought you were headed home."

Trace shrugged out of his thick wool coat and tossed it onto the bar as he passed. "You know I can't leave you with all this."

"Of course you can," Walker argued. "That's why you pay me."

"Yes, I pay you, but I don't ever want you to think I'm taking advantage of how hard you work." He plopped down on the loveseat beside Walker. "Pass a stack to me."

Walker pushed some papers his way. "Are the roads bad? You were gone a while."

"Nah," Trace answered, only half listening as he shuffled through the receipts. "I had a call to make. I've been in the parking lot for about half an hour."

A soft chuckle escaped Walker. "A half-hour conversation at three in the morning. What's his name?" Before Trace had time to answer, Walker snapped his fingers. "Ten bucks says it's the same guy you watched the door for all night."

Trace pulled a face and laughed. "I'm not sure that's a fair bet, since you're betting against the person who actually knows, but yes. It was the same guy. His name is Hunter."

Walker sucked in a hiss. "My cousin's name is Hunter. Don't mess with my cousin. He's a loser."

As Walker no doubt hoped, Trace barked out a laugh. "I seriously doubt it's your cousin."

"Well, how do you know?" Walker asked, turning ridiculous. "You haven't asked. It might be Hunter. He can be pretty charming up until he's stealing your truck."

Trace's shoulders shook. "Unless your cousin is Lane's dad, then it's not him."

Walker's smile fell. "Seriously? You're chatting up Lane's dad?"

"Yep." Trace wasn't ashamed and had no plans to start.

"If he's Lane's dad, he's definitely old enough to be your dad."

Trace shrugged. "He's not Lane's biological father. Hunter adopted Lane after marrying his mom, but yeah, he's probably old enough to be my dad."

"Wait," Walker said, holding up one hand. "He's old enough to be your dad, he's drug-addict Lane's father, and he's married to a woman."

"Technically, he's a widower."

"But he was married to a woman."

Trace glanced over and met Walker's stare. He'd never seen the man get this worked up over anything, and he'd broken up some pretty epic fights in the club. "I'm not understanding your tone. You do realize most people are way more sexually fluid than they'd like to admit, right? I mean, I've dated women too. As to his age, who the fuck cares?"

Walker blinked. "Well, goddamn. If I'd known you didn't care about age, I would've tried to win you a long time ago."

Trace snorted. Walker was older than him, but not ridiculously so. He was only thirty-nine. That wasn't what struck Trace as funny. "No, you wouldn't have. We work together."

"You're right," Walker said, going back to matching up receipts with the night's numbers. "I need this job too bad. If it weren't for that, though."

A smile tugged at Trace's lips and he leaned into Walker. The guy was huge and like a human heater. Walker might've been his employee, but he was also Trace's friend, and Trace loved him like family. Without Walker, he wouldn't have Club Incubus. The guy handled everything right alongside Trace. He was a grumbly bear. He let a minute pass before giving his thoughts away. "For what it's worth, if we didn't work together, I might let you win me."

Walker kissed his forehead and went back to work. It was one of those moments that truly relaxed Trace, making everything else fall away. Walker was one of those people. Trace would rather sit with him in silence than most people at their brightest.

Chapter Three

Trace was oddly nervous, which went against his usual shameless personality. Although Hunter had said Lane was aware, it felt a bit strange going to Lane's house to pick up the man's dad. Of course, Hell would freeze before Trace ever admitted as much to Hunter. He needed Hunter relaxed. Hunter met him at the door. The moment thcir gazes met, a blush touched Hunter's cheeks. Like that, Trace was back on solid ground.

"I didn't see Lane's car," Trace said as Hunter pushed open the screen door for him.

Hunter nodded. "Someone showed up this morning and took his car in for new tires. He was gone the moment they brought it back."

Trace pulled the door closed behind him. "That's good. I don't have to worry over any witnesses when I do this, then." He towed Hunter forward and claimed his mouth. To Trace's surprise, he was the one who found his back against the door. He loved the way Hunter kissed. One moment, it was deep and searching. The next, his kiss turned sweet and soft. Trace found himself clinging to Hunter's shirt and holding him in place. He'd never been more scared of a moment ending. Hunter leaned away but kept his eyes closed. Trace memorized every detail of Hunter's face. He was beautiful. Clean-shaven and hardened jaw. Even Hunter's nose was perfect. It was like he'd been sculpted. His eyes opened. Heat blasted Trace.

The blush was back. "Sorry. I've been thinking about that all day." Hunter tried taking a step back.

Trace held tight. "Don't apologize. I've been impatient too." Trace held Hunter's stare as he used the man's shirt to slowly lure him back into their kiss. Hunter lowered his head. Trace bumped his lips against Hunter's, taking his time, tempting him. Their tongues met, teasing before Trace retreated again. Still, he didn't release his grip on Hunter. He changed angles, bumping the man's chin with his lips. Trace wanted him frustrated and craving more. "I'm taking you to dinner, because you deserve it, but I really want to take you to bed instead." He needed Hunter to know he was desired.

Hunter stroked Trace's hips, drawing him closer. "I'm cool to skip dinner."

The door opened behind Trace, whacking him in the back. They leapt away. Lane poured inside. "Oh, good. You're here." Lane barely spared them a glance. He was too busy staring at a crumpled paper in his hands that looked as if it had seen better days. "While I was waiting on a friend earlier, I had some thoughts on the club. Just some observations I made last night that would increase your sales. I wrote them down." He passed the paper Trace's way. "Feel free to take them with a grain of salt, but you know I bounce around to all the clubs and I see stuff that works for other people. Normally, I wouldn't share anyone else's methods, but we're friends."

Trace glanced at the list. It was random words scribbled in no particular order. He wasn't sure if he was meant to make sense of the so-called list or if Lane planned to explain. "Fresh garnishes."

Lane's head bobbed. "You know, ginger and cucumber. Stuff like that. I've noticed, at places that add a touch of fresh ingredients in drinks, they get more orders. A lot of the fancy drinks people ordered last night, they stuck with one. I think having that extra something fresh makes them feel like they're sticking to their diet or some shit. Put a slice of cucumber in a five-thousand-calorie drink and they'll buy them all night."

That was actually genius. Trace smiled. "You're amazing." Which reminded Trace. "To give you something to think about, I'd love for you to come onboard full time. You could implement your ideas and you're always a huge help."

"Nah," Lane said, waving off Trace's offer. "I like the changing scenery. Otherwise, I get bored or wear out my welcome. You're my friend. That's why I was thinking over ideas to help. We can go over the list and just use what you want."

Trace looked over the crazily written jumble of ideas. Something niggled at the back of his mind. Trace had seen this level of over-enthusiasm before. He met Lane's stare. The guy was practically jumping in place. "How often do you do things like this?" he asked, nodding toward the piece of scrap paper.

"All the time," Lane said, looking in every direction and not focusing on any one thing. "I have tons of ideas about all sorts of things. In my room, I have stacks of notebooks on different topics. Mostly I concentrate on my plans for a dispensary. It'll be huge if I ever get the money to get started. Weed is a winning lotto ticket right now."

Trace chewed his bottom lip. His gaze moved between Lane and Hunter. Hunter's face was set—like he fought to keep his thoughts hidden or he hoped he didn't explode. Trace thought it was a good time to make a break for it before Hunter lost his shit. "We were about to go to dinner."

"Oh," Lane said, finally focusing on Trace. He looked between them. "Oh." This time, he sounded like realization dawned. "That's cool. We can discuss this later."

Guilt hit Trace like a sledgehammer. Lane didn't seem to care, but he felt disloyal all of a sudden. "Would you like to join us?"

"No. No, man," he said with a laugh. "That's weird." Lane looked horrified by his own words. "I don't mean this is weird," he clarified, motioning between Trace and Hunter. "That's adorable and I'm thrilled. I meant, it's awkward to be a third wheel. Don't worry about me. I can find something to get into. What is this? Sunday? I can find something."

"Walker works Sunday nights. You could swing by the club and go through your list with him." Walker would fucking kill him.

Lane brightened. "I might do that." He gave Trace a sharp nod. "I'll do that." He felt of his light blond hair, which stood in every direction as if he'd been running his fingers through it. "First, I need a shower. You two have fun and don't do anything I wouldn't do."

Trace chuckled. "So we're pretty much free to do whatever."

Lane brightened. "Exactly." Without a word of goodbye, Lane took off down the hall. Hunter watched him go. Trace watched Hunter. His expression hadn't changed. A muscle in his jaw worked overtime. Trace took his hand and led him out the door before Hunter decided to chase Lane. His silence was unnerving as they climbed inside Trace's SUV. Trace couldn't take it.

"Say it before your brain pops."

Hunter glanced over as he snapped his seatbelt in place. "Say what?"

Trace didn't let Hunter pretend nothing happened. "Whatever you've been thinking since Lane showed up. You look like you're chewing off your tongue."

Hunter shook his head and looked away. "My son's biggest dream is to be a professional drug dealer. I'm not sure what I'm supposed to say about that one."

Trace brought Hunter's hand to his mouth. For a moment, he held Hunter's hand to his lips while he picked his words. "You're doing great. Lane is... a unique soul," Trace said, settling on a description. "He dreams big. Whether you see it or not, you did a great job. Now all you can do is let him be."

Hunter stared at him in silence for a long moment. Finally, a small smile touched his lips. "You're an old soul, aren't you?"

"Maybe so." Trace knew he should put the car in gear and take Hunter to eat. He couldn't look away from Hunter's sexy eyes. "Or maybe I just want to ease your mind so you can focus on me."

Hunter didn't break their eye contact. He looked every bit as interested in

Trace as Trace was in him. "You have my attention. This should feel awkward."

"It doesn't."

Hunter fingered the neck of Trace's shirt before using the bit of material to lure Trace closer. "It doesn't," Hunter agreed as he touched his lips to Trace's.

There was an odd tugging sensation in Trace's chest. He wanted to know Hunter's every thought. Most of all, he couldn't wait for more of this—intimate moments and too soft kisses.

Holy shit. Trace was awesome. Hunter kept thinking about what he'd almost missed. Hunter had truly expected it to feel weird going on a date with another man after so many years of marriage. Trace made feeling uncomfortable impossible. He was funny and charming. Trace was also sensual. His every glance was heated. His touches calculated. Hunter didn't think he'd looked away one time all night.

What had started as a normal date had quickly morphed into the most romantic night of Hunter's life and Hunter didn't think Trace was even trying. The restaurant had been packed with an hour and a half wait. Trace had spoken quietly to a few people, and fifteen minutes later, they'd left with a takeout order. Ten minutes after that, Trace had Hunter ensconced at a tiny table by the fireplace in his cabin. Hunter listened while Trace told story after story about growing up with two dads who were both horrible at disciplining him. To Hunter, it sounded more like Trace had been born with the devil's charm and used it every chance he could. In fact, Trace was so bewitching, Hunter didn't know how he'd gone from sitting at the table to curled beneath a blanket on the couch with Trace in his lap. All Hunter knew was Trace smelled like candy. Hunter kept inhaling deeply.

Trace shifted in his lap, getting comfortable with his back against the arm of the couch. He stared at Hunter. His gaze moved over Hunter's face as if trying to solve a puzzle. "You have amazing eyes."

Hunter fought the urge to dismiss Trace's compliment. He'd never been good at accepting praise. "They're nothing compared to yours." He wasn't simply turning the conversation from himself. Trace's eyes were the most amazing shade of blue. They made Hunter think of staring at the ocean on a tropical island somewhere. He felt at peace while staring into Trace's eyes.

Trace shook his head. "You must not look in the mirror often. Lots of people have blue eyes. I'm average in almost every way. You have something unique. I can't stop staring and trying to figure out exactly what it is."

It hit Hunter. For all Trace's charm and confidence, he didn't know he was extraordinary. He didn't see the way he wowed people with his beauty. Hunter didn't know how to make Trace see what he did. With no plan other than the need to touch Trace as much as possible, Hunter stroked Trace's stomach. His fingers found the hem of Trace's shirt and slipped beneath. Trace's skin was soft and smooth. "Maybe what you're seeing isn't a physical thing. Instead, you're seeing my fascination with you flashing in my eyes."

Trace's eyes fell closed. His nostrils flared slightly as Hunter dipped one finger inside the waistband of Trace's jeans and stroked. Hunter hadn't meant the move as sexual. In truth, he hadn't thought at all. He just wanted to touch Trace. Be closer to him. With Trace's eyes closed, it seemed the most natural thing to lower his head and brush his lips across Trace's. He immediately pulled away.

"I'll have to go home soon. Tomorrow is a workday for me."

"In a minute," Trace said, shifting to his knees and straddling Hunter's lap. He buried his fingers in Hunter's hair, massaging his scalp. "I won't keep you up too late." He kissed the corner of Hunter's mouth. His voice dropped to a whisper. "Thanks for taking a chance on me. I know you have doubts." Trace changed angles and kissed the other corner of Hunter's mouth. Hunter was hypnotized. "You won't be disappointed," Trace promised. His tongue swiped Hunter's bottom lip. Hunter chased after him. He forgot his need for sleep. His brain stopped working altogether. Trace let Hunter catch him. Their tongues stroked. It was a playful kiss and hot enough to singe Hunter's skin. Trace had something most people lacked. Hunter couldn't decide what it was, but he wanted to touch it. He massaged every place he could reach and kissed as deep as he could get. Trace's touch softened until their lips barely brushed. He had Hunter chasing him again. This time, he didn't let Hunter have his way. Instead, he slipped from Hunter's lap and held out his hand.

"Come on. I'll take you home."

He was so fucking beautiful. Hunter didn't take his hand right away. For a moment, he was struck immobile by the vision Trace presented. His hair was a sexy mess from Hunter running his fingers through it. His light blue eyes shone bright with lust and youth. He looked like God had created a miracle on his best day. There was no reason whatsoever for him to look at Hunter the way he was now—like no other man existed.

Hunter took Trace's hand and stood. He hated the reality of needing sleep. Hunter resented being human and the necessities that came along with that. All he wanted was more Trace. He wasn't sure Trace would call again. This might've been a fluke. Hunter hadn't done anything to wow Trace. He wasn't sure he should. Whatever this was, it didn't stand much of a chance. Hunter had too many years on Trace. He had too many issues. It wasn't right for him to become anyone's burden. Still, there was a selfish part of his heart that clung to hope. Maybe something good would happen to him for once. Trace made him believe.

———ele———

Trace: *I made it home safely.*

Hunter: *Good. I wouldn't have been able sleep without hearing from you.*

Trace: *You don't have to worry. Get some sleep. I don't want you driving to work tired.*

Hunter: *Goodnight.*

Trace: *Goodnight.*

Hunter: *I had a good time tonight.*

Trace: *I did too. See me again?*

Hunter: *We'll figure something out.*

Trace: *Okay.*

KINKY BABY

—ele—

Trace: *I met someone nice.*

Dad: *I don't think you've ever told me about anyone you've met. Who is this mystery person?*

Trace: *Just someone nice, but I don't think he likes me as much as I like him. He didn't try to sleep with me, and he doesn't sound overly thrilled about seeing me again.*

Dad: *Run. He's straight.*

Trace: *I don't think so. Not really anyway. He kissed me. I just don't think he really likes me, you know?*

Dad: *Run. He's stupid.*

Trace: *Did Jake like you immediately?*

Dad: *Yes. He just needed me to tell him to like me.*

Trace: *What about Dad?*

Dad: *Your dad was unique. Sometimes, you remind me so much of him. Don't give this guy too much of yourself, okay? It's okay for someone to make you chase them a little. Your ego could use the exercise, but don't let him change who you are, because you're pretty damn special. I'm not saying that just because I'm your dad. You have a spark a lot of people are missing. Don't let him steal that.*

Trace: *I love you. Tell Jake I love him too.*

Dad: *I will. I love you too.*

Dad: *Also, you make sure this guy knows if he breaks your heart, I'll break his kneecaps.*

———ele———

Hunter: *Lane disappeared an hour ago, telling me not to wait up. How do you feel about me making you dinner?*

Trace: *I would love that. What time should I be there and what do you need me to bring?*

Hunter: *Just bring yourself and now, if you're not doing anything.*

—— *ele* ——

Trace: *Thank you again for dinner. I had a nice time.*

Hunter: *Me too. I didn't mean to run you off by mentioning I have to work tomorrow.*

Trace: *It's okay. I know you need your sleep.*

Hunter: *Still. Maybe we can do something this weekend.*

Trace: *It would have to be during the day. I work Friday and Saturday nights.*

Hunter: *We'll work something out.*

Trace: *This guy really doesn't like me. I don't know why I keep trying and he keeps calling.*

Dad: *Maybe he's not as brave as you. Not everyone is, you know.*

Trace: *Maybe. I'll give it one more date. I really do like him.*

Trace: *You cooked last. It's my turn. Lunch?*

Hunter: *Just tell me when and I'm there.*

Trace: *I'm ready whenever you are.*

Hunter: *Putting my shoes on now.*

Trace: *Good. I'm ready to see you.*

Hunter: *Same.*

Being good sucked. Hunter's brain was so fogged with unquenched lust he couldn't function. Trace was a temptation Hunter had never been taught to fight. The thing was, he liked Trace. A lot. He'd never expected to meet someone like Trace. Hunter didn't want Trace to think he only wanted sex. Dear god, he did, though. Trace was sexy and nice. He was funny and charming. The guy kissed like Hunter wouldn't walk straight again after a night with him. Hunter made it through a dinner and a lunch without tackling Trace to the floor. He wouldn't make it through another date. Hunter didn't make a conscious decision not to try. When Trace opened the door, wearing a blue t-shirt that matched his eyes to perfection, and smiled, showing off his sweet side, something inside Hunter snapped.

He ate Trace alive with his gaze as he stepped through the door. Trace's lips parted as if surprised by Hunter's sudden intensity. Hunter bided his time, stalking his prey and waiting until Trace closed the door behind him. The instant they were shut away, Hunter's hands found Trace's hips. He crowded Trace's space.

Trace licked his lips while Hunter watched with hunger in his heart. "I wasn't completely honest about lunch," Trace said, sounding nervous. "I don't cook."

"That's fine," Hunter said, walking Trace slowly backward, and maneuvering him toward the bedroom.

Trace flattened his palms against Hunter's biceps and stroked. "I figured

I'd wait until you got here, and we could choose some takeout together."

Hunter nodded, even though he had no plans to do any such thing. "I vote we skip that and go to bed instead."

Trace's lips slowly twisted into a teasing smirk. "Damn. I didn't get a kiss or anything?"

A hint of Hunter's bravery fled. Looking at the situation from Trace's point of view, he must have sounded like an entitled ass. "Sorry. You deserve b—"

Trace covered his mouth, cutting off his apology. "Stop. I was joking." Trace inched closer. Hunter took a breath. Trace was gorgeous, and Hunter was nervous as hell. "I'm going to uncover your mouth now. No more talking." Trace's fingers slipped away. Hunter locked his back teeth to stop himself from apologizing. "Good boy," Trace whispered as he touched his lips to Hunter's. It was a sweet, innocent kiss. Trace's arms encircled Hunter's neck. The final space between them disappeared. He could feel Trace's erection. His cock stirred. The air grew heavy. Trace didn't rush. "Tell me why you're nervous so I can fix it."

Until Trace made the accurate assumption, Hunter hadn't realized how completely terrified he was. "Too many reasons to count."

"Pick a place to start. I'll help." He backed up a step and stole Hunter's shirt without preamble. "Is it because I'm a man?"

Hunter blinked, still trying to decide exactly how he'd lost an article of clothing so fast. "I guess that's part of the reason." The words swiftly died on Hunter's tongue as Trace stripped away his own shirt. "Goddamn."

Trace was perfect. It wasn't fair. He was skinny but toned. Tight and sleek. Trace eyed Hunter like he was equally impressed. His fingers skimmed down Hunter's ribs. Without warning, he dipped low and unbuttoned Hunter's jeans. In the process, he lightly caressed Hunter's crown, nearly hobbling him. "Is it because I'm younger than you'd like me to be?"

"I don't remember what we're talking about."

Trace smiled. "Good." He turned and walked away.

Hunter watched him go. His brain took its sweet time catching up. It wasn't until Trace cleared his bedroom door and his pants dipped, flashing part of his perfect round ass, that Hunter's feet unfroze from the floor. He chased after the sexy globes. Trace stripped while Hunter watched. Water filled his mouth as Trace peeled the jeans from his body. Hunter's hands automatically dropped to his unbuttoned jeans. He shoved his zipper down and stroked his cock, incapable of taking the pressure.

After setting one knee on the bed, Trace glanced over his shoulder. "Are you only wanting a show, or do you plan to join me?"

Hunter was across the room and covering Trace's body in seconds. While Trace was completely nude, Hunter pretty much fell on the guy with his dick out. He kissed and bit every place he could reach. Trace moaned like he was already getting fucked while he held tightly to his comforter. Hunter dragged his teeth down Trace's spine until he could sink them into the gorgeous ass that kept him mesmerized more than what could be considered healthy. He was rougher than he meant to be. Hunter couldn't stop or slow. Trace drove him insane in more ways than one. Hunter kissed the small of Trace's back and shoved his thighs apart.

"Condom," Trace cried before Hunter went too far. "Top drawer." The fact that Trace sounded every bit as desperate as Hunter felt kept Hunter on the edge of insanity. He ripped the drawer open with so much force, he moved the entire side table six inches. He found a condom and tore it open with more enthusiasm than needed. His hands shook as he rolled the sheath down his length. He fell on Trace again, determined to ease the madness. "Lube," Trace yelled before Hunter could hurt him.

This time, a growl escaped Hunter as he dove for the side table. He found the tube and squirted the shit every-where, soaking his jeans that he still hadn't removed. Hunter gave no fucks. He wanted Trace's ass now. He fingered Trace's asshole with lube. His stomach muscles cramped at the hot tightness of Trace. Hunter knew he should slow down. He was too far gone. Trace was a temptation Hunter had never been faced with before. If this was a test, he'd failed because his crown was already pushing past the tight ring of muscles and sinking into Trace's heat. A soft cry escaped Trace—like a whimper. The sound ripped at Hunter's soul. He froze. His mind cleared enough to make him panic. He'd probably really hurt Trace in his crazed rush.

Hunter pulled out. "I'm sorry."

Trace smacked the bed. "Why in the fuck are you stopping?"

It hit Hunter. Trace's cry had been in pleasure. Hunter shoved his jeans down past his knees, grabbed Trace's hips, and shoved his way back inside. Trace cried out. Hunter rocked against him and Trace pushed back, taking him. His ass tried sucking Hunter deeper. Hunter had never been this close to blowing this fast. Everything felt too good. Trace was too responsive. It was the single most mind-blowing experience of his life. Hunter pounded Trace's ass, scooting them across the bed in his enthusiasm. Trace clawed at the covers, biting the bedding and moaning. Hunter absorbed every detail. He committed every sound to memory.

"Mmmm. Hunter. Oh my god. I'm going to come."

"Fuck," Hunter moaned, because he hadn't thought Trace could get hotter.

"Holy shit, baby. I can't hold back. You're hitting the right spot." Trace's body went taut. His ass squeezed Hunter's dick so tight, he gasped, stuck somewhere between pleasure and pain. Then the first spasm hit. Trace's ass convulsed, sucking hard on Hunter's dick, pulling him deep. Without warning, an orgasm slammed into Hunter, tearing a long string of curses from his throat. He forgot every word no sooner than it left his lips. Nothing registered but the way his body popped with waves of pure ecstasy. He collapsed, squashing Trace to the mattress beneath his weight. Hunter wheezed as he sucked air. There was nothing sexy about him in that moment. Trace had wrecked him in a way he'd never experienced. Because his heart needed more, Hunter gently rolled off Trace. He was covered in cum and sweat. His skin was flushed, making his light blue eyes seem even lighter. He was the sexiest man Hunter had ever set eyes on. Hunter kissed him. Actually, it was more like he opened his mouth over Trace's bottom lip and held it between his lips. He still hadn't caught his breath. Hunter just needed to have his lips on Trace's. His heart demanded it. Trace's hand covered his, making Hunter realize he'd been stroking Trace's side. He'd obviously found a ticklish spot.

He chuckled against Trace's lips. "It's too late. I know now and I'm filing that tidbit away for future use."

Trace huffed. Even that sound was sexy.

"We made a mess."

Trace nodded. "We should definitely strip the bed once my legs work again."

Hunter couldn't stop smiling. No matter how hard he tried smoothing out his features, his lips stretched once again. "I'm not in any hurry."

A tired-sounding chuckle rumbled from Trace. His smile immediately fell. "Don't laugh, okay?"

"Why would I laugh?"

Trace bit his lip, looking embarrassed. Hunter's stomach muscles clenched with desire. He'd just had Trace. It wasn't enough. Hunter feared he'd never have enough of Trace. "I thought you didn't like me." A blush touched Trace's cheeks at the confession. Hunter couldn't look away. "Why would you think that?"

Trace shrugged. "Before today, you've kind of rushed me along—like you couldn't get away fast enough. There's a part of me expecting it to happen right now."

It was Hunter's turn to fight a wave of embarrassment. He cleared his throat. "Um, actually, I've been rushing you along so I wouldn't embarrass myself by falling on you like a man who's been celibate for three years, which I ended up doing anyway. I'm not going anywhere."

Trace cocked his head and eyed Hunter. "Have you been celibate for three years?"

Hunter's gaze skirted away. "Maybe." His face scrunched up in thought before he realized what he'd done and smoothed out his features. "Actually, it's probably a lot longer, because Lacy was really sick for a long time." He shook his head, feeling stupid. "You don't want to hear about that, and I shouldn't be talking about it right now especially." He cuddled closer to Trace. The smell of Trace's expensive cologne—like chocolate and cherries—overcame Hunter. He buried his face against Trace's throat and inhaled. His eyes fell closed. Without thought, his lips brushed Trace's skin. He felt full for the first time in forever. Happy.

Trace ran his fingers through Hunter's hair. When he spoke, his words vibrated against Hunter's lips, which were still pressed against his throat. "I like hearing about your life. You didn't burst into existence the moment you met me. I get that you had years and years of living before me."

A laugh escaped Hunter. "Years and years, huh? I know I'm old." He leaned away. Trace's eyes shone bright with humor, making him realize Trace was teasing.

Trace's features softened. "I'm glad the problem wasn't you not liking me. Because I like you a lot."

Hunter wondered if Trace knew how incredibly fucking brave he was. Every second Hunter spent in his presence, he felt luckier to have met him. "I like you a lot too. It probably goes without saying, but I want to keep seeing you. You probably have your pick of men, but I'm hoping you'll choose me. Can I stick around until you need to leave for work?"

"I'd love for you to stay longer than that. Come to work with me. I'll show you off to the world."

"How about some middle ground? What if I'm waiting when you get home?"

"I'll take it."

Hunter felt the first kernel of hope for a beautiful future burst to life. For the first time in ages, he didn't think about all he'd lost, stood to lose, and couldn't control. There was nothing but the person in front of him, staring at him in a way he could get used to. He wanted more.

While Hunter showered, Trace stared at the ceiling. His body hummed with happiness. It had been one of the best days of his life. There were still a few hours left before he needed to be at the club. He wished he didn't have to go, but he couldn't call in and leave Walker hanging with no warning. His gaze slid back to the bathroom door. Fuck. Hunter was amazing. Trace had known he would be, but then again, he hadn't. Nothing could've prepared him for the way Hunter moved him. He'd been rough and then loving. Playful and then serious as sin. Trace wanted to invade every corner of the man's life and set up shop. A chuckle escaped Trace. He'd definitely been dicked down. If he didn't watch out, Hunter would break him and steal his heart. It wasn't like Trace to be this doe-eyed.

The bathroom door opened, and Hunter stepped out. Trace tried not to swallow his tongue. He couldn't lift his gaze from the outline of Hunter's thick cock in his wet towel. He'd had that. It was good dick. The porterhouse of penis.

"What time do you need to leave?"

Trace scooted closer to the edge of the bed. He couldn't resist touching Hunter. "When I'm ready." He reached out and loosened Hunter's towel, letting it drop to the floor. "There's no rush."

Hunter looked wicked as he smirked and set one knee on the bed. "Did you have something else in mind?"

Trace bit his bottom lip and waited. His gaze slid down Hunter's body. His thick cock stirred beneath Trace's stare.

"Goddamn. How do you do that?"

Trace's guilty gaze shot back to Hunter's face. "Do what?" Even to Trace's ears, he sounded overly innocent.

"Make me insane with need with just a look," Hunter said, straddling Trace's body. He sat back on his heels, pinning Trace to the bed beneath his weight.

Trace shrugged. "It's not how I'm looking at you. It's who I'm looking at." He trailed his fingers down Hunter's stomach until he reached Hunter's cock. He played the innocent again. "I don't know what to do. You should guide me."

Hunter shook his head as if trying to break a spell. Still, his dick hardened in Trace's hand. "That shouldn't be sexy, but it's you."

Trace didn't stop. "Come on, Daddy. Tell me how to make you happy."

"I am fucking ecstatic already because I have you."

Trace's act fell away. "You're right. You do have me. Let me make you scream."

For a moment, Hunter stared down at him in silence. "Jesus, you're beautiful."

With a light tug, Trace urged Hunter higher. "Let me lick you. My mouth is already watering."

Hunter shifted positions and led his cock to Trace's lips. He swept his crown across Trace's bottom lip. Trace's tongue shot out, tasting. A low moan filled the air. Trace lost the will to tease. He sucked Hunter down his throat. The move seemed to flip a switch in Hunter. He snapped. With one hand braced on the headboard, Hunter fucked Trace's mouth. He took what he wanted. His hips rolled as he pounded at Trace's throat. Trace didn't back down. He hadn't lied when he'd told Hunter he loved sucking dick. It was a power trip. Right now, whether Hunter realized it, Trace owned him. Trace took control. He pulled away and jacked Hunter's cock while he sucked on the man's balls. The sound of Hunter gasping for each breath bounced off the walls. Trace urged him higher, spreading Hunter's cheeks and stabbing at the man's asshole with his tongue.

"Oh, god." The cry sounded ragged. Trace's chest swelled with pride. Hunter tugged at his hair, making his scalp burn. Trace licked and sucked, intentionally driving Hunter insane. By the time Trace was sucking Hunter's dick again, Hunter had lost all semblance of control. His motions were frantic. The sounds he made were inhuman. Even after hot cum overflowed from Trace's mouth and the cries died away, Trace didn't stop until Hunter collapsed. Hunter curled into a panting heap beside him. He stared at Trace, wearing an expression Trace couldn't decipher. Trace's chest felt full and tight. Heavy with emotion. There was something about those hazel eyes.

"You're the only good part of my life."

Hunter's claim took Trace's breath. His eyes stung. He hated that Hunter was unhappy. "Tell me how I can make your life easier."

Hunter shook his head. "Just keep showing up."

"You got it." He wasn't going anywhere. They had something. Trace didn't know what yet, but he planned to find out. Until then, he'd keep his eyes wide open. Hunter might claim he didn't need more, but Trace would judge for himself. He kind of liked the idea of playing the superhero. Maybe he'd get to save Hunter from the ugliness he endured.

Chapter Four

HUNTER: *I MISS YOU.*

Trace: *I miss you too.*

Hunter: *This child will be the death of me.*

Trace: *Who? Lane?*

Hunter: *Yes. He's passed out on the kitchen floor. He's still breathing so I'm leaving him.*

Trace: *I want to say it'll be okay.*

Hunter: *But we both know that's not true.*

Trace: *Tell me what I can do to make it better.*

Hunter: *You are making better. I don't have anyone else to talk to.*

Trace: *Surely I can do more. Back rub? Booty massage? Blow job?*

Hunter: *LOL! You're amazing. Have I told you that lately?*

Trace: *I don't know. Maybe I need to hear it in person.*

Hunter: *I'll be there in ten.*

—ele—

Trace: *You should come to my club tonight. I'll buy you drinks. You know, wine you before I dine on you.*

Hunter: *I don't want to bug you at work. Come see me after.*

Trace: *This is hardly a normal job and I'm the boss. Come see me.*

Hunter: *Come after. I'll make it worth your while.*

Trace: *Okay.*

Hunter: *Damn. I can't wait.*

Hunter: *What time do you get off?*

Trace: *I'll probably leave here around 2. Why?*

Hunter: *Lane is destroying his room, so I'm headed your way. If you don't care, I'll sit in your driveway until you get home.*

Trace: *Come to the club. It's too cold to hang out in my driveway.*

Hunter: *Nightclubs are loud, and my mood is shit. I kind of just want to sit in the silence and stop shaking.*

Trace: *Okay. I'll let Walker know I'm leaving.*

Hunter: *You don't have to do that. I'm good. Just being close to your place makes me feel like things aren't a complete wreck.*

Trace: *I've got you, sexy.*

—— *ell* ——

Trace: *Can I take you to dinner before I go to work? There's an awesome place where you need reservations, but I know the owner.*

Hunter: *Why don't we stay in instead?*

Trace: *Are you ashamed to be seen with me? You never want to go anywhere. I'm not complaining. It's just... odd—like you don't want to be seen with me.*

Hunter: *No. It's not that. I'm selfish. I want you to myself.*

Trace: *Oh. Okay. I'll pick us up takeout.*

Hunter: *Thanks.*

———ell———

Trace: *Have you ever dated anyone who didn't want to go out? BTW, don't tell Dad about this text.*

Jake: *I won't tell. What's going on? Who doesn't want to be seen with you?*

Trace: *See? That's not even what I said, and it's not in my head. He doesn't want to be seen with me. What the hell?*

Jake: *I probably read too much into your text. No one in their right mind would be ashamed to be with you. Maybe he's tired or is an introvert?*

Trace: *I don't know. I just feel... I don't know. Insecure, maybe? I think I'm in love with this guy.*

Jake: *Wow. Well, love does tend to make people overthink, especially when you're in that stage where you don't know if they feel the same way.*

Trace: *Did you tell Dad first or did he tell you?*

Jake: *He told me, and then I told him by text the next day because I'm a chicken shit.*

Trace: *You're adorable. I love you.*

Jake: *I love you too. It'll work out. {{HUGS}}*

As always, being with Hunter stole any doubts Trace had about them. When they were together, tucked away in their own little bubble, they were perfect.

The roses Hunter had waiting for Trace sat on the bedside table. Trace's gaze moved their way. His heart squeezed in his chest. They were red. They were the sort of gift people gave when they were in love. Hope was a heady thing. Trace continued massaging Hunter's back. He was almost certain Hunter was half asleep. Trace couldn't stop babying him. Oil coated the man's skin. He looked sexy between Trace's thighs. Nothing sucked harder than leaving when Hunter looked as he did now—like Trace could just stay forever and they'd never mention how they'd ended up permanently living together. Fuck. He wanted that too badly. Three months of dating Hunter had fucked with his head.

Trace lowered his head and kissed a path down Hunter's spine before retracing his steps, kissing up his back. "I have to make an appearance at the club tonight. Walker needs me." Trace ensured his lips brushed the spot between Hunter's shoulder blades with every syllable. He hated leaving Hunter like this. Trace already missed him. He couldn't stop kissing Hunter, hoping to seduce him into feeling the same. "You should come with me."

Hunter released a loud sigh. "I don't think that's a good idea."

Trace froze. Hunter could have said any number of things. He was too tired. Trace had worn him out. Anything. Instead, he said it wasn't a good idea. In other words, he didn't want to be seen in public with Trace—just as Trace feared. Trace rolled from the bed without a word. He tugged on his clothes without looking Hunter's way.

"Trace."

Trace pretended not to hear. There was nothing to say.

"Don't leave mad."

Hunter's words made the situation so much worse. His demand proved Hunter knew what he'd done. Hunter's refusal to be seen in public with Trace was a purposeful act and not in Trace's head. They were fuck buddies and nothing more. The only one in love was him.

"I'm not mad." Trace wasn't sure if that was a lie. Not that it mattered. Trace pulled his shirt on before focusing on Hunter. Hunter stared at him with those goddamn hazel eyes that had stolen Trace's heart and all Trace felt was done. Sometimes it sucked that he knew his self-worth. "My dad said my ego could use the exercise of chasing someone, but damn, I never expected to be constantly begging someone to be seen with me. Maybe you'd be happier with some-one else. Someone you're not ashamed to be seen with."

Hunter rolled and sat up. He looked wounded. Trace wished it didn't hurt. "Is that what you want? For me to be with someone else?"

The rage was real. Hunter hadn't tried pretending Trace was wrong. He hadn't acted the wounded lover, accused of feeling something he didn't feel. He was more ashamed of being with Trace than he was about Trace knowing it. "This isn't a matter of preferences. You can't stand the idea of anyone know-ing you're with me. I won't be your se-cret shame. I deserve better. If you don't know it, then I've made an even bigger mistake by ever touching you than I'm already thinking I did."

Trace imagined Hunter's expression would be the same if Trace slapped him. He'd like to cry—beg to know how they'd gone from making love to this, but they'd been inching here from the first time their eyes met. Trace had seen this coming from the very start. He'd wanted Hunter too badly to stop. Now he would pay the price for his selfishness.

"Trace, you're younger than my son." He sounded desperate.

Trace felt nothing. "Don't leave out the part about me being a guy. That's an issue too."

Hunter glanced away.

Trace shook his head. An ugly-sounding snort escaped him without permission, followed by a strangled-sounding chuckle. He turned away. There wasn't a goddamn thing funny about the situation. It was no one's fault but his. Hunter had tried telling Trace from the beginning he wasn't interested. Trace was the one who'd kept chasing Hunter, despite the warning signs, until Hunter gave in. He shook his head again as he walked away. Trace didn't know anything any longer, except that he was a goddamn idiot. A fact that surprised no one, Trace was sure. Either Hunter would call again or he wouldn't. Whatever. Maybe next time, Trace would make Hunter beg for his time for once.

—ell—

Hunter lasted all of an hour after Trace left before the guilt sent him to the shower. He fucking hated nightclubs. Wasn't it bad enough that he lived with someone who was always drunk or high? Trace was his safe place from all that. Now he felt like—if he didn't go at least once—Trace would soon get sick of him and move on to someone younger, hotter, and more flexible. He didn't want to lose Trace. Trace was the only good part of him. Fuck. He couldn't keep sending Trace away, looking wounded and rejected. That shit made his chest hurt.

All the way to Club Incubus, Hunter cursed under his breath and massaged the ache in his chest. Trace might really be done with him already. Hunter didn't have anyone else to blame. Why hadn't he argued and told Trace he wasn't ashamed? All because he didn't want to go out. Fuck. He didn't understand why it bothered Trace so much that he was just fucking exhausted. Goddamn it. He couldn't lose Trace.

A groan escaped him when Club Incubus came into view. The place was slammed. There were zero parking spaces. Cars were lined up along both sides of the street. Hunter parked behind the farthest one. With his head down, he made his way to the door. There was a huge dude checking IDs. He looked unfriendly as hell. Every time Trace talked about Walker, there was so much love in his voice, Hunter pictured someone totally different. This mountain of a man wasn't anything like that image.

"ID."

Hunter dug out his wallet. "I'm here for Trace."

Walker snorted. "Yeah? You and everyone else inside. Good luck." He glanced down at Hunter's license and then met his gaze again. His expression underwent a few subtle changes. "So you're Hunter?"

"I'm Hunter." He wanted to go home.

He handed Hunter's license back. "Trace will hound me until the end of time if I charge you the cover."

"I'm willing to pay." Anything. He just needed to get to Trace and make sure they were okay. He was already dating way outside his league.

Walker shook his head. "It's cool. Have fun." Without another word, he motioned for the next person in line to move forward.

Hunter shook his head and went inside. Walker hadn't been unfriendly, but Hunter got the feeling they wouldn't be friends. Great. He was winning right and left tonight. As he stepped through the door, everything else fell away. Trace owned all of this. It was hard for Hunter to wrap his mind around it. At home, Trace was... well, Trace was more amazing than anyone Hunter had ever encountered, but this place left Hunter reeling. Trace didn't need him. For anything. Trace lived in a tiny cabin. He didn't feel untouchable there. Here, Hunter felt the chasm between them harder than ever before. The place was huge. Lights flashed in time with music. People danced at the bar, grinding on others. Mirrors and liquor bottles lined the walls behind bars on each side of the room. Even with two bars, people were still crowding each one, vying for the bartenders' attention. The place was so packed, Hunter could barely breathe. Even with bodies packing every inch, Hunter spotted Trace immediately—like the boy wore a homing beacon. Strobe lights flashed above him. The music pulsed. Bodies gyrated. Trace seemed to be the only person who was completely still. On a loveseat, in what looked to be the VIP lounge with the dance floor as its backdrop, and with one booted foot resting against the edge of a table, Trace sat alone with a bottle of water balanced on his bent knee. Trace glowered at nothing. His dark expression seemed at such odds with his usual bubbly attitude. Goddamn, the boy was beautiful. Hunter didn't want to feel the way he felt. He didn't want this ache in his gut that only Trace soothed. It was only a matter of time before Trace realized Hunter wasn't worth his time. Hunter very much feared Trace had already made that connection.

His feet moved in Trace's direction. A young, much-sexier-than-Hunter guy dropped into the empty space next to Trace. Hunter froze. It seemed he'd been right in thinking this was a mistake. As he looked on, the sexy new arrival leaned close and spoke against Trace's ear. Trace didn't turn his head. He didn't acknowledge the guy at all.

Trace sipped his water, looking to all the world like he still sat alone. Hunter moved closer without thought. Trace's gaze shifted Hunter's way. The young hottie at his side stroked Trace's stomach, trying harder to snag Trace's attention.

Trace finally glanced the boy's way. "You're in his seat," Trace yelled to be heard over the music, nodding toward Hunter.

A shot of pride hit Hunter alongside a hint of pity for the guy's embarrassment over getting dismissed. But damn, Trace had a way of making Hunter feel like there was no one else—like he was special, even when he was angry with Hunter, as he was now. The boy shot Hunter an annoyed look before scurrying away. Hunter moved to fill the spot he'd vacated. Trace leaned his way. Their shoulders met. Hunter linked his fingers through Trace's. They didn't speak. Trace pressed a quick kiss to Hunter's shoulder, and all was right in Hunter's world again. They would be fine. Trace would see. Hunter would try harder.

Chapter Five

THEY HADN'T MOVED FROM each other's company since Trace left the
club with Hunter the night before. All
night, they'd made love. Then they'd
made breakfast while stealing touches.
Trace had lounged in Hunter's lap and
watched movies all day before they'd
gone back to hiding in bed when Lane
rolled out of his. Hunter felt more playful than usual. Having Trace's forgive-
ness buoyed his hope and his mood. He
carefully avoided making eye contact

with the clock because he didn't want Trace to leave again.

Trace looked sexy as sin beneath him while Hunter straddled Trace's hips. Still, Trace tried getting away. Hunter licked the tip of Trace's nose for the fifth time. With his arms pinned to the bed, Trace couldn't get away from Hunter. "Ewww. Stop. Oh my god." Every cried word was barely distinguishable through Trace's laughter. Hunter's stomach hurt from spending the past hour laughing while he wrestled with Trace, torturing him with licks and kisses.

Trace's laughter was sexy as hell. Hunter couldn't get enough. Trace tried lifting his hips again and bucking Hunter off, but Hunter was too heavy and refused to budge. Hunter's laughter died away. The wiggling beneath him had him going hard. Trace's expression turned heated, proving he felt the same. Trace fell still as Hunter held his stare and lowered his head. He didn't close his eyes until after his mouth covered Trace's. He didn't want to miss seeing a moment of Trace. Hunter had never been happier. His chest felt like it might explode. He was in love with Trace. There was no doubt. Even he didn't know exactly when it happened or why. Before Lacy, Hunter had dated a few men, but those dates had never gone far. Hunter wasn't the type to feel a spark with just anyone, much less this inferno that burned with Trace. Hunter couldn't get enough of Trace's kisses. His heated glances set Hunter's skin ablaze. Maybe he'd fallen for this reason right here—days of being tucked away and solely focused on each other. No matter the hows or whys, Hunter needed Trace. Wanted everything with him. Right now, he just wished Trace wouldn't leave again.

Hunter wasn't ready to go back to reality where he worked a job he hated, barely paid his bills, and his son was an addict.

"Stay," Hunter begged, sounding desperate even to his ears.

"Come to the club with me," Trace countered.

A loud groan escaped Hunter before he could call it back. "No," Hunter said, playfully dragging out the word and trying to take the bite from his first reaction. "Please don't make me. I'm so tired."

Trace's smile didn't abate, but his eyes lost some of their happiness. "Oh. Okay."

"Oh, baby," Hunter said, keeping his tone light as he stayed locked in Trace's space. "Please don't be mad. I hate that we're on opposite schedules too."

"I'm not mad."

No. He wasn't. Trace was disappointed, and that was so much worse. Hunter couldn't turn back the hands of time and be twenty years younger. Guilt was a heavy thing. "You should stop wasting your time on me. It's not fair for you to be stuck with someone who can't always do the things you do."

Trace shook his head. Hunter couldn't get a read on his mood. "Can't or won't?" Trace swiped his hand through the air, wiping away the question. "Don't answer that. Never mind. You're right. You work during the day and you can't be out all night. It's not fair of me to want you with me all the time."

Damn. Now he felt twice as bad. "I want to be with you all the time too. I'm sorry my life is such a mess and I'm barely paying my bills. Otherwise, I'd quit my job and follow you everywhere, clinging and driving you nuts until you begged me to stop. I'd tell every guy who tried hitting on you that you're mine and they need to back off. You'd start to wonder if you need a restraining order, but then I'd promise to change. I'd—"

"Stop," Trace said, laughing and trying to cover Hunter's mouth. Hunter pressed a kiss to Trace's palm. Trace touched Hunter's jaw and lured him closer. "I was being greedy. It happens sometimes. Don't think about it again. Maybe one night next weekend, you can come. If not," Trace shrugged, "then, oh well. I'd still rather be with you than anyone with all the time in the world to spare." He brushed a kiss across Hunter's lips. "Don't think about it again."

Hunter tried letting it go. There was a huge age gap between them. If they wanted to make this work, they'd have times when it felt like it didn't and stay together anyhow. That was life. "I think you should kiss me some more before you go," Hunter whispered, trying to recapture the mood. They had another hour or so before Trace had to go. He didn't want to spend it talking. They were so beautiful together. He didn't want Trace to ever think otherwise. Hunter just needed Trace to stay.

—ele—

Trace tried his damnedest not to think as he watched couples swaying to a slow song. Hunter had shown up last night. Trace shouldn't want more. Sometimes, he felt like this whiny, needy ass who wasn't happy unless he got his way. Hunter was tired. Trace needed to meet him halfway. Damn, it was hard watching couples dancing so close with Hunter missing from his side. All Trace wanted was to skip out and curl up in bed with his man. He missed Hunter's heat, his laughter, and his kisses. Trace swallowed the desire to run for the door. He wanted to go home.

"Why do you look so sad?" Lane asked, appearing at the edge of the lounge. He crawled onto the loveseat and put his head in Trace's lap.

Trace ran his fingers through Lane's hair, distracting himself as he watched Lane's eyes fall closed. "Why aren't you behind the bar? Have you already run out of things to do?"

Lane shrugged. Trace felt more than saw the motion. "They ran me off, saying I'm too messed up to be working tonight. Maybe they're right. I do tend to fuck up a lot when I'm like this."

While massaging Lane's scalp, Trace picked through his words, hoping he didn't upset Lane. "Baby, have you ever considered talking to the doctor about this? I think you might be bi-polar."

Lane peeked one eye open. "That's an odd thing to say. Why do you think that?"

Trace continued running his fingers through Lane's hair while keeping his voice level. "I could be wrong. I'm not a doctor. It's just the way you talked about your stacks of notes and not stopping until you've got all your ideas catalogued. The way you throw yourself into everything you do. It reminds me of someone I used to know a long time ago. He would have these manic episodes and become a huge overachiever, needing to set his every idea into motion. If you're staying high to lessen those racing impulses, maybe there's more to it. Just a thought."

Lane was so still, Trace wondered if he'd fallen asleep. After a moment, Lane nodded. "The next time I see the doctor, I'll mention it. You never answered my question, though. Why are you sad?"

Trace shrugged, even though Lane's eyes were closed. "I thought your dad might make a surprise appearance again tonight. Guess not." Even Trace heard the disappointment in his voice. He'd thought they'd moved past Hunter's shame. Hunter said he was tired, but it felt like more. It just felt like something else and this feeling eating at his gut was driving him nuts. Sometimes, they felt miles apart—like they weren't in sync. Trace didn't know how to bridge the gap. Maybe it was his fault. He'd yet to admit how much he loved Hunter. Maybe that would matter. Maybe not.

When Lane finally responded, his words slurred, and he sounded more asleep than awake. "He's a homebody. Dad likes his quiet time. Don't take it personally. He likes you a lot. I'm so glad I convinced him to take one for the team."

Trace blinked. He wasn't sure he'd heard that last bit correctly. "What do you mean take one for the team?"

Lane rolled onto his back and covered his eyes with his arm and kicked his legs over the arm of the couch. "The night you two met," Lane said so low Trace had to lower his chin to hear Lane's mumbling. He was so fucking thankful the club was closing and quiet. Otherwise, he wouldn't have heard a word of any of this. "I saw you kiss him. Dad said he wasn't interested. I told him you're rich. He's about to lose the house and I need a backer for my dispensary. So he took one for the team."

Trace's eyebrows shot up. He sucked in a breath as the blow landed, and then his lungs gave out beneath the pain. No wonder Hunter never came to the club. He probably saw Trace working as a mini vacation from his ploy. Trace had never used anyone for anything in his life. Maybe that was why he hadn't seen it coming when it happened to him. The way Hunter looked at him—like he loved Trace—flashed through Trace's mind. He'd kissed and touched Trace like he cared. It had felt so real. Trace sucked in a gasp as his head spun from lack of oxygen. His heartbeat pounded inside his ears. For a moment, Trace wondered if he'd faint. He needed to get out of here. There was a real possibility he would soon fly apart. Lane was out. Trace slipped from beneath his head and made a break for the door. Walker tried stepping into his path, making Trace wonder if he looked as wrecked as he felt. Trace shook his head and stepped around him. He would text Walker later and explain. Right now, he couldn't. Hunter had made a fool of him. Broken him. Trace had thought they were real. He'd known they had obstacles to overcome, but Trace had truly believed they were working together toward something real. The whole time, Hunter had been sacrificing himself for a payout. Trace sat behind the wheel inside his Range Rover, staring at and seeing nothing. He wanted... Trace rubbed at the ache in his chest. He wanted what he'd thought they'd been, but it wasn't real. The anger hit next—like a truck slamming into his brain. His heart hardened. In that moment, Trace vowed to never love again.

Chapter Six

HUNTER STARED AT THE corner where the walls met the ceiling. His mind stayed elsewhere. Somewhere it was safe from the insanity beating at his mind's walls. Surely he had things to say, actions he could take, or something that needed doing. Instead, he sat and stared at nothing. Hunter could only recall one other time he'd been this scared of his emotions. Terrified they would demolish his soul. The day Lacy died, he'd felt the same, and he'd thought this empty chasm inside him would never heal.

They'd been together eighteen years. He'd been tied to Lacy through marriage, a child, and a million little things. Losing Trace shouldn't feel the same on any level. Yet here he was again.

Lane slinked into the room, squinting against the light like a vampire. He looked like hell. The dark smudges around his bloodshot eyes gave the false impression Lane hadn't slept in ages. In truth, it was six at night and he was just now waking for the day. Hunter wanted to feel something—outrage. Anything for his son's upcoming funeral, because Hunter knew sooner or later, Lane would turn up dead. Hunter felt nothing beyond exhausted. He couldn't help Lane. Hunter was tired of trying.

"You're home."

Hunter didn't respond to Lane's asinine observation. His throat hurt too bad from swallowing the silent screams.

Lane peered closer at the grandfather clock. "Shit. Is it six at night or in the morning?"

"Night."

At his croaked answer, Lane looked his way. "What's wrong with your voice?"

Hunter held up a letter for him. "This is for you."

Lane crossed the room and plucked the sealed envelope from Hunter. He ripped it open and had to catch a slip of paper that tried falling out as he unfolded the letter. Hunter already knew what it was. There'd been a similar one in his letter. Lane's eyes moved from side to side, silently reading. His expression went through all the emotions. He looked between the letter and the slip of paper and back again.

Hunter didn't give him time to say whatever was in his head. He held up his envelope. "I have one too. Would you like to swap?"

They switched. Hunter's gaze moved over Lane's letter. It said as much as he'd expected.

Lane,

If you'd wanted my help with your business idea, all you had to do was ask. It wasn't necessary to try to break me by enlisting your father. I've enclosed a check to cover your startup costs. This isn't a loan. I don't want the money back. All I ask in exchange is that neither you nor your father darken my door again. — Trace

Hunter eyed the check. It was for fifty thousand. Hunter hoped the money brought Lane much happiness. That was exactly how much this check had stolen from Hunter. He set Lane's envelope on the table and waited for Lane to hand his back. For a long moment, Lane held Hunter's letter and stared at nothing. Hunter lost his patience and took it back. He'd read it at least ten times, trying to make the words make sense. Since Hunter still hadn't found an answer, he read the note again.

Hunter,

I want to be angry and say lots of hateful things. It seems, even in my time of need, I don't know how to hurt anyone. Since day one, you've been uncomfortable with dating me. I knew it. You haven't really tried hiding it. That's the only reason I never offered to help when you said you were having a hard time paying your bills. You haven't seemed open to inviting me any farther into your life. I guess I thought if I kept showing up, you'd decide you loved me and then I'd be free to give you everything. All I can do now is hope that your plan to "take one for the team" didn't include making me fall in love with you before you crushed me, because I can't believe you'd be that cruel. But maybe I'm wrong. It seems I was mistaken about a lot of things. I guess I know now why you acted like it was horrible to be with me anywhere other than the bedroom. It really was horrible for you. I asked you not to laugh when I told you I was worried you didn't like me. You didn't laugh. Not aloud. But now I know you were laughing on the inside over my foolishness. The thing is, I'm not the joke here, because I know I gave you a real shot. Everybody's looking for the one, but nobody's trying to be the one. I tried to be the one for you, and I hate myself for wasting a piece of myself on you. So take this as a sorry-for-forcing-my-attention-where-it-wasn't-wanted gift. Just because I mean nothing to you, that doesn't mean you meant nothing to me. I don't want you to lose the house you shared with Lacy. Plus, eventually, you'll probably have to help pay to put Lane through rehab. Hopefully, this check will help. Have a nice life, gorgeous. It was never an act for me. —Trace

Hunter's gaze moved to the two-hundred-and-fifty-thousand-dollar check included with the note. Somewhere in the world, there was a twenty-year-old boy who'd been destroyed by an older man who should've never touched him, and Hunter would never, ever forgive himself. It didn't matter he hadn't been using Trace. Equally, it mattered not at all that he'd fallen head over heels for Trace. He'd still been guilty of much of what Trace accused him of doing. He might've shown up once to Club Incubus and publicly held Trace's hand, but—deep down—Hunter knew the truth. He'd only done it so that would be the end of the discussion on the matter. Hunter hadn't been proving a point that he wasn't ashamed. He'd been hoping to silence Trace's valid fears. The truth of it was—Hunter was the monster Trace believed him to be.

Lane cleared his throat, reminding Hunter he wasn't sitting alone in the pile of shit he'd created. "I might have told him that," Lane said, sounding like his throat hurt. "I really don't remember. Last night was..."

Hunter stood. He couldn't do this today. Maybe he couldn't do this at all anymore. He'd wondered a million times if he was making Lane worse. If he was enabling him. "No doubt, last night was like every night." Even to Hunter's ears, he sounded tired and broken. Hunter set the letter and check aside. There wasn't a single chance in hell Hunter would be cashing that check. Lane would probably cash his, and—just like with everything else in Lane's life—there wasn't a damn thing Hunter could do to stop him. But Hunter wouldn't hang around to watch it. Surely there was something else he should be doing. He wouldn't darken Trace's door. Trace had asked him not to. But Hunter also couldn't stay here a second longer. Unlike Trace, Hunter couldn't leave himself. Trace could get away from Hunter and all this bullshit. Hunter was stuck with himself forever. Maybe Lane was the smart one. Perhaps being a drugged-out idiot was the answer he'd been searching for. Anything was better than being Hunter. Anything at all.

Lane stormed the door to Club Incubus. He'd shown up with no real plan other than begging. Lane would do anything. He couldn't stand his dad looking at him the way he'd looked at Lane before disappearing. Lane had fucked up many times in his life. His dad had never been done with him before. Lane feared that he was this time. Completely and utterly finished. Walker stepped into his path before he cleared the door. "You've been banned."

"What?" The loud screech assailed Lane's ears before he realized he was the one who'd made the sound. He cupped his pounding head. "Sorry. What?" he asked, this time in a normal voice.

"You've been banned. Trace said if you showed up to let you know you'd gotten what you wanted and there's no need to come back."

"I didn't get what I wanted."

Walker's eyebrows shot up. "Seriously? Fifty thousand for your start-up and your dad's house paid off wasn't enough? You need to go. I don't know why Trace let you extort money from him, but I'm not Trace." Even the muscles in Walker's face flexed, letting Lane know Walker wouldn't hesitate to get physical.

The thing was, Walker didn't know him. Not really. Lane had no pride. If he got his ass kicked, oh well. He hadn't stopped constantly being in pain for a good ten years, at least. "I just need to talk to him. My dad loves Trace. All this is on me. I need to tell him. Dad wasn't using him. I was just high and talking shit. This is my fault."

Walker shrugged, looking unaffected. "It wouldn't matter if you weren't banned; he's not here, so move along."

Lane felt his face screw up in confusion. Trace was always here. "Do you know where he is? This is important. My dad already has to live with knowing I'm a fuck up. I can't mess this up too. I have to tell Trace."

"Can't help ya," Walker said, motioning for the person behind Lane to step forward so he could check their ID. "You're holding up the line, Lane."

"I'll hold it up all night," Lane yelled before he could stop himself. He cupped his head again. Goddamn migraines. No matter how much he smoked, they didn't go away. He couldn't even feel his lips, but his fucking head wouldn't stop pounding. When the dizziness passed, he met Walker's stare again. "What do I need to do to pry Trace's whereabouts from you? I'll do anything." Lane dragged his gaze down Walker's body. "Anything."

A loud snort sounded from Walker. His light brown eyes swam with mirth. "Feel free to take this personally: guys who think they're straight suck in bed."

If Lane had been clear-minded, he might've taken Walker's insult to heart. Luckily, Lane had lots of fun drugs swimming through his system. He shook his head. "I've got to be honest. I'm probably way too high to get it up," he said, waving off Walker's claim. "But my mouth still works."

Walker let out a bark of laughter. "If there's anything straight men suck at more than sex, it's giving head. Sorry, dude. Not interested."

For some reason, Walker's claim stung. Lane shook it off. "Not what I meant. I meant I can and will stand here all night talking nonstop until you tell me where I can find Trace."

Looking unfazed, Walker shrugged. His giant, muscular shoulders lifted and fell, fascinating Lane for reasons he couldn't pinpoint. "You're wasting your time. He went back to California. That's all I know. I don't have an address or anything like that. So, really, I can't help you."

A smile exploded across Lane's face. He didn't have an address either, but he had bread crumbs. "Cool. Thanks." He turned to leave. A vise-like grip on his upper arm almost ripped him off his feet. His gaze followed the line of the arm holding him until he met Walker's stare. Worry etched the man's features. "Don't drive, okay?"

"I don't have a choice. Being as how there's no way in hell I'd ever take Trace's money, I can't afford to get to California any other way."

Walker turned his gaze to the sky as if praying for patience. "Fuck my life," he growled, pulling a two-way radio off his belt. "Mario, I need someone else at the door. I have to run an errand."

A static-filled answer Lane couldn't make out came through the device. Walker obviously understood. With a sharp nod, he waved Lane toward the lot. "Let's go."

Lane blinked in surprise. "Go where? You're not taking me to California."

Walker snagged his arm and marched him toward a large truck that sat higher than seemed normal. "I'm putting you on a plane. From there, you're on your own. No way am I trusting a junkie with cab money."

"I'm not a junkie," Lane muttered. Even to his ears, he sounded resentful. "If anything, I'm a stoner. It's not at all the same."

Walker froze and met his stare. "Look me in the eyes and tell me there's nothing but pot swimming through your system right now."

Lane eyes skirted away.

Walker snorted. "And you thought I'd want to fuck you."

Ouch. Goddamn. That hurt more than Lane expected. Halfway to the airport, Lane lost the battle against the discomfort of the silence. "What did you mean earlier when you said guys who think they're straight? Do you not think I'm straight?"

Walker chuckled. It did something to Lane's stomach he couldn't understand. "The moment you get the least bit of chemical courage in you, you start crawling all over Trace. Is that why you ruined his relationship with your dad?"

A shot of outrage ran through Lane. "That was an accident, but I think you're projecting. How long have you been in love with Trace?"

"I've loved Trace since the first time I met him." Walker flashed him a smile. "Just like everyone else who meets him. Don't think I didn't notice you dodging. Maybe you stay high because that's the only time you can do what you really want without hating yourself."

The silence dragged on again. Lane stared at nothing. Did he care about Trace? Yes, but he didn't think it went beyond friendship. Lane wasn't particularly sexual. In truth, he didn't think about being with anyone. He had too many other problems. "I live in constant pain," Lane said, admitting something he never talked about. "That's why I stay in a haze. I'm not chasing the high. I can't take the pain."

"So see a doctor."

Resentment overwhelmed Lane, the way it did every time Lane thought about it. "I've been to the doctor. They send me home with creams or antidepressants. When you don't know what's wrong with you, it's all in your head, or you're just looking for pain killers. They don't know where else to start when you don't know how to explain that you're in extreme pain, all over, and it's crippling. They test your thyroid and then stop calling. You're forced to book appointment after appointment with no relief. It's a money pit and disheartening to the point you need the damn antidepressants to cope with their shit." Lane's hands lifted and dropped to his lap in helpless defeat. "I get that it's easy for you to judge, but you don't know what you'd do in my shoes. I have two choices—self medicate or kill myself, because no one is helping me."

Lane stared out the passenger side window and ignored Walker for the rest of the drive. It had been a damn long time since anyone had managed to get under his skin and leave him outraged. No one understood what it was like to curl up in bed, writhing in pain with no hope. Since shortly after turning sixteen, he'd dealt with this invisible monster that constantly flayed him alive. He was beyond giving a fuck what judgey people like Walker thought of him. Lane balled his hands into fists, fighting the rage. Fuck Walker. Lane didn't understand why he cared what Walker thought. It wasn't fair to be trapped in this body and have to explain why it had driven him to the brink. Why did he care?

"Trace's dad and stepdad own a bookstore called Baby Boy's Books. It's on Main Street. Trace hangs out with them while they work during the day. That's where you're most likely to find him."

Lane looked Walker's way. Walker was staring at the road like his life depended on it. "Thank you. For everything," Lane tacked on, because—despite everything—Lane recognized Walker didn't have to help him at all.

Walker dipped his chin. "Despite all signs pointing to the contrary, you're not completely horrible."

The claim surprised a bark of laughter from Lane. "You're not as dull and unfeeling as I thought."

Another delicious-sounding chuckle filled the cab of the truck, making Lane smile. Maybe Lane hadn't completely fucked up his life after all. There was a warm tremor of hope vibrating through him. Maybe he would try living again someday. Maybe.

Chapter Seven

THE SMELL OF BOOKS and cupcakes didn't soothe him the way Trace had hoped. His dad was out of town and there was no one he could ask for advice. Not that he planned to tell his dad much. There was a real possibility his dad would really go break Hunter's kneecaps. Trace didn't want that. He wanted the ache in his chest to go away. He wanted to text Hunter and see the man's name appear on his phone. Trace wished he could go back a few days. He missed the warmth of Hunter's hugs and his scent. No one had ever taught him to hate. Logically, he knew he should curse Hunter's name and key his car. Whatever people did when they found out everything was a lie. Instead, Trace sulked. He followed Jake's brother Easton around the bakery attached to the bookstore.

Easton kept feeding him and Trace kept accepting because he didn't know how else to fill the yawning void inside him. Easton was oddly comforting. The man was pure drama in a thousand-dollar shoes, but he was strong and a survivor. Being near him made Trace feel like he could be strong too. Deep scars lined one side of Easton's face, left behind from an attack no one ever talked about. They did nothing to take away from Easton's beauty. Twenty-nine, blond haired and green-eyed, Easton was like a tiny sprite. Men took one look at Easton and wanted to save him. Easton never looked at any man anymore.

After an hour of Trace crowding his space, Easton finally broke. "What brings you to town, sweetie? I know it's not to visit your dad. He's not scheduled to return from taking my baby brother on an overdue honeymoon for two more weeks."

Trace shrugged as he ripped the plastic from a sucker and popped it in his mouth. "I guess you could say I got my heart broken, and I don't want to be alone."

Easton glanced away from the cupcakes he was decorating. "You? Who would hurt you? You're so sweet."

That was nice, especially coming from Easton. The man wasn't known for dishing out compliments. He was sassy and high maintenance. At least, he showed hints of those traits occasionally. Trace hadn't met Easton before the attack. Trace thought Easton was beautiful, but Easton didn't always sparkle, thanks to being touched by something ugly.

Trace shook his head, forcing his thoughts back on track. "I've been seeing someone for a few months. For about half a minute, I thought he might be the one. I was not his one, it seems." Trace winced. "Turns out he was only interested in my money."

Easton hissed. "You need to find you an older man. The young ones are too much trouble. No offense. You're not like anyone else. You have an old man's soul."

"Thanks for that, I think, but he was older. He's forty-two."

"Damn," Easton said, dragging out the word. "You dated an older man, *and* he's poor? Sacrilege."

Trace shrugged. "It doesn't matter now. Lesson learned. I should've seen it coming, really. He never wanted to go out. I kept telling myself he was tired, and it had nothing to do with him being embarrassed of me. Guess I was wrong about a lot of things."

"Listen to Auntie on this one."

"You're barely my uncle by a technicality, but whatever," Trace muttered under his breath.

Easton didn't slow. "Even though I've given up dating, I'm an expert at dating older men. They are past all the bullshit of the younger generation. Older men have moved beyond going to clubs and dealing with someone all the other men chase. Oh, and men who don't know where they want eat. They hate that, but that's another story. Anyhow, if you're dating an older man, they'll want to eat at home, where they can relax. They'll want you there with them because they're not too old to enjoy your fine wares. Above all else, you have to make sure they always know you only have eyes for them."

Trace shook his head at Easton's complete inability to listen to a word anyone else said. "That's not even the issue here."

"It's not the only one," Easton chirped like he still hadn't really heard Trace. "Whereas I only dated rich men, you are the rich man in this equation. All this guy has is his boring old self to offer, while you have it all—youth, money, and popularity."

"I'm boring," Trace mumbled, sounding like a child and not caring. Easton wasn't listening anyhow.

"No," Easton argued. "You are sunshine, rainbows, and cherry lollipops." Easton punctuated his claim by snatching the sucker from Trace's mouth and booping Trace's nose with it. He kept talking like nothing happened while Trace scrubbed at the sticky candy on the tip of his nose. "Not only does this guy not have the ability to spoil your sexy ass, he has to deal with working all day and knowing all the younger, sleeker models want to take you home for a test drive from that club of yours. He's tired."

Trace growled. "I work all the time too. I'm tired."

"Are you?" Easton asked as sarcastically as possible. "Or were you at the club all night, partying right alongside your customers? Because I'm here to tell you, sweetheart, that's nowhere near the same as working at a job you hate all day, only to come home and still can't pay your bills."

"What would you know about that?" Trace asked while adding a healthy dose of eye roll. Easton had been raised with money too. He'd never gone without.

Easton popped the sucker back in Trace's mouth. "I know how to date older men. You're still learning."

"For fuck's sake. He was *using me for my money*. You're talking at cross purposes with me. We never had a problem with me being sunshine and rainbows."

"Are you sure? Because I'm not. I don't date anymore, but if I did, I'd know that I can't keep going out partying and expect an older man to be happy with me."

"Oh my god. Why do I even talk—" A movement at the door caught Trace's eye, distracting him. Lane pushed his way inside while looking at something behind him. Trace made a dash for it, hiding behind the closest rack of books. He watched as Lane made a beeline for Easton. Trace was close enough to hear every word, but the tall metal rack kept him hidden from sight.

"What the—Welcome to Easton's. How can I help you?" Easton asked, turning a bright smile on Lane and abandoning his quest to find out why Trace had leapt behind the closest book rack.

"I'm looking for Trace Thomson."

"You should buy a cupcake instead."

Lane shook his head. "No, thank you. I'm just looking for Trace."

Easton lifted one eyebrow at Lane, making Trace proud they were related, even if it was only by marriage. "First, you buy a cupcake. Then, I tell you where Trace is." Trace recognized the stubborn tilt to Easton's jaw. He bit back a laugh.

A loud sigh escaped Lane. He dug his wallet out. "Fine. How much?"

A luminous smile stretched Easton's face. "Four fifty. Which flavor do you want?"

Lane eyed the counter for half a second before waving in the direction of a fluffy pink creation. "That thing, I guess." Lane paid and waited until he had the cupcake in hand before pushing again. "Now. Where's Trace?"

"He's right behind you."

Trace fought a growl at being sold out. He should've known Easton had a price, and it wasn't high.

Trace stepped out from behind the book rack. "Lane." Even Trace heard the resentment in his voice. "Did you run the numbers and decide fifty grand wasn't enough?"

"Fifty grand really isn't that much," Easton said, chiming in.

Trace shot him a dirty look. "It is when you're twenty-five and still living with your dad."

"Oh, in that case, yeah. You should take the money and run."

Lane stared at Easton with his eyebrows raised until he looked away and pretended to clean.

"I tore up your check," Lane said, handing Trace an envelope with tiny bits of his check inside. "You're my friend. I don't want your money."

"We're not friends." Trace tried handing back the envelope in case Lane wanted to tape the check back together.

Lane wouldn't take it. "Yes, we are. At least, you're my friend anyway. I know I'm a shit friend, but I do care about you. You can't listen to me when I'm high. Granted, I don't know exactly what I said, but I can guess, and I'm a fucking idiot. My dad loves you. He's incapable of using anyone, especially you. Your relationship was real. I'm the fake. Not him. Hate me. He didn't do anything."

"I plan to hate you both, but thanks for the offer." Trace was incapable of not being a smartass with his heart in tatters.

"Why?" Lane asked, sounding desperate. "It wasn't true. I say a lot of stupid shit. That's not his fault. He didn't do anything wrong."

Trace rubbed his chest. There should've been elation at Lane's confession. Trace didn't feel better. The idea of going back to Hunter didn't make him happy. He should've been happy.

Easton made a gesture behind Lane, snagging Trace's attention. "Younger, sleeker model," Easton mouthed while pointing at Lane's back.

Trace's gaze moved between the two. A light switch flipped in his brain. Fuck him, Easton was right. In some con-voluted roundabout way, Easton recog-nized what Trace hadn't. Hunter and he were too far apart in too many ways. Trace's business meant Trace had to be out late, partying with customers, and keeping them happy. Sometimes that meant men flirted with Trace. Hunter didn't want that life. But that wasn't all; Hunter didn't want him. Not really. Maybe he desired Trace, but he was ashamed of his lust—tired from working or not. Trace didn't want to go back to being with someone who was embarrassed to be seen with him. He loved Hunter, but he wasn't sure he liked him.

It also didn't escape his notice that Hunter hadn't been the one who came after him. No matter what Lane said, Trace had a bad feeling Hunter was relieved it was over. Trace swallowed. He was tired of feeling like he couldn't breathe around the lump in his throat. Trace had come to California to get away from this. He needed some space.

Trace shook his head. "I'm sorry you came all this way for nothing. There's just too much standing between your dad and me."

Lane's shoulders fell. "You're my friend. It's not for nothing." He sounded so broken that Trace's eyes burned. Lane turned away and focused on Easton. "Do you have any water to wash this down? I guess I'll eat my cupcake while I try to figure out how I'm getting home."

A growl rose in Trace's throat. Sometimes he hated that he cared about people. "How did you get here in the first place?"

Lane barely spared him a glance as he picked at the paper around his cake. "Walker put me on a plane last night and I slept in the airport. From there, I took a cab. I just gave this guy right here my last five dollars," he said, nodding toward Easton.

"Easton."

Lane looked away from his cupcake long enough to focus on Easton at Easton's interruption. "What?"

"My name is Easton," Easton supplied. "Not 'this guy.'"

"Oh." Lane went back to staring at his hands.

Trace had never seen anyone look more defeated. He tilted his chin up and stared at the ceiling, praying for strength before focusing on Lane once more. "Come on."

Lane licked his icing before looking Trace's way. "What?"

"Come on," Trace repeated, motioning toward the door. "We can go to my parents' house. You can borrow their shower and I have clothes there. We'll fly back together."

Lane shook his head, being stubborn. "That's okay. I'll figure it out. Maybe it's best I just stay here and find some work. I think my dad is done with me this time."

Trace's eyes burned unexpectedly. Everything was so fucked up. "I'm not done with you."

Lane looked away, blinking. He sat in silence for a moment before clearing his throat. "Okay." With his head down, Lane followed him to the door. Trace held it open for him and cast one last look Easton's way. Easton gave him a smile obviously meant to encourage him. Trace wished it did. Right now, nothing felt like it would ever be good or right again.

Chapter Eight

A MONTH WITHOUT HUNTER didn't ease anything. He got up and went to work, but it felt like something was always missing. Lane still worked bar back for him and came to hang out when he didn't have a job for the night. Trace felt stupid for always being so happy to see him, but it felt like he still had a piece of Hunter when Lane was around. He shouldn't want it, but he did.

In his usual spot, on the loveseat at Club Incubus, Trace played with Lane's hair where it rested against the back of the loveseat. It was getting long and unruly. Trace couldn't resist the soft locks. Lane let it go on, making Trace wonder if he was starved for affection. Trace didn't doubt Lane's lifestyle had driven away most people in his life. He couldn't be happy living like this. Trace cared too much to stay silent.

"Are you sober tonight?"

Lane pulled a face. "Unfortunately."

His grumbly answer made Trace smile despite the conversation they needed to have. "I love you."

Lane's sweet smile made the confession worthwhile. "I love you too."

"Good. I have a proposal for you."

"Oh no. Don't propose. You dated my dad."

Trace swatted his knee and squeezed. "Be serious for half a minute. I need your full attention. I want you to go to rehab. On my dime, of course. If you'll do this for me for a minimum of three months, I'll help you start your dispensary."

Lane held his tongue until Trace finished before shooting him down. "No. It's not that I'm not interested. I don't ever want you to think again that I hang around for what you can do for me. You're my friend. Let's leave it at that."

"Oh, don't think this is charity. It'll be a partnership. I'll take half the profits until you can buy me out. The rehab is also for my benefit. I don't want to do business with a junkie."

"I'm not a junkie," Lane said with a heavy sigh.

Walker cut in. "Do this, Lane. If you agree, I'll go to your doctor appointments with you and be your intimidation factor until they find the cause of your mystery pains. We won't let you live in misery. We just want you healthy."

Lane stared at Walker in a way Trace couldn't decipher. Trace was fascinated. "Are you serious?" Lane sounded like there was no way Walker was serious—like no one would do something like for him.

"Of course. There has to be a legitimate reason for you to always be in pain. I won't stop pushing until they find it because there's no way in hell I'd let you suffer. But you have to get off the drugs. This is no way to live."

Lane's gaze moved between them. For a moment, Trace wondered if Lane would cry. "Okay. I'm in."

Trace fought back a cheer. They hadn't won yet. Going to rehab didn't automatically mean Lane would succeed. For the rest of his life, Lane would struggle. Trace didn't give two shits about the pot, but everything else needed to go. Otherwise, Trace didn't expect Lane would live another five years. Trace moved to his feet. "We should dance."

With a laugh, Lane stood. "Damn, you'll start a stampede of men trying to get to you. I'm game." He glanced Walker's way. "What about you, Walker? You want to show the young ones how daddies get it done?"

Walker rolled his eyes but shifted to his feet. "I can't let you two get molested on the dance floor. Let's go."

A laugh rose in Trace's throat as he hit the dance floor. It was the first time since losing Hunter that he'd felt like smiling. He bounced to the music and moved his hips, acting his age for once. The smiles Walker and Lane wore drove him to act a fool. The emotions inside him still didn't feel quite like happiness, but he didn't feel as hollow as usual. He danced to every song, carefully avoiding the hands of other men, and allowing Walker to cut them off until a slow song filled the air. Trace froze. To his surprise, Walker and Lane paired up. They moved to the music, still smiling and laughing while talking close to each other's ears.

Trace took two steps, determined to sit back down. Hands slid across his hips, drawing him back against a chest he'd know anywhere. Hunter's familiar scent overwhelmed him. Trace's eyes fell closed as he automatically matched the beat to the music. For a moment, they swayed together like that—Trace's back against Hunter's chest. Hunter turned Trace in his arms. Trace wound his arms around Hunter's neck without a thought. His mind stayed blank. Trace's body was on autopilot. There wasn't an inch between them. Not a word was spoken. Three slow songs played in a row. They never spoke or broke contact. At one point, Hunter's lips brushed Trace's neck and goosebumps rose on Trace's skin. Trace loved him. It seemed that love hadn't budged an inch.

A fast song came on and Hunter kissed his neck one final time. They went their separate ways. Trace headed for his office. He didn't know how to feel, but he needed to be alone. The next night, Hunter showed again. Once again, he didn't say a word, but he danced every slow song with Trace. For three weeks, every night Club Incubus was open, Hunter showed. Trace always knew exactly where Hunter was every second of the night. He could feel Hunter's eyes upon him. Hunter didn't try to win him back. Each night was the same—slow dances and soft kisses against Trace's throat or nape. Trace knew Hunter had to be tired. Staying out late all the time and working all day had to be kicking his ass. That was why when the fourth Friday rolled around, Trace stayed home.

To say Hunter was bone weary would be the understatement of the millennium. He hadn't slept more than two hours at a time since coming home to Trace's letter. There were dark circles under his eyes, and he'd lost twenty pounds. He felt twenty years older. The only thing keeping him going was the fact that Trace wasn't throwing him out of Incubus. As long as Trace kept walking into his arms for every slow dance, Hunter would keep showing up.

He'd taken a month to think about things. Actually, it had only taken him three days to figure out he couldn't live without Trace. He'd spent the rest of the month trying to decide if Trace was better off without him. In the end, his heart won. Maybe Trace would never take him back. If he did, Hunter would spend the rest of his life ensuring Trace needed him too. He planned to be that amazing because Trace fucking deserved it.

Hunter tried not to drag his feet as he made his way to the door at Incubus. Only his excitement over seeing Trace kept him moving. His legs felt heavy from exhaustion. Walker caught his eye.

He expected the club's manager slash bouncer would nod and wave him inside as he'd done for the past three weeks. Instead, he reached out, stopping Hunter.

"Trace isn't here." Hunter's heart leapt into his throat. Had Trace finally decided he was done? Hunter couldn't deal. Walker made a calming gesture, as if he read Hunter's mind. "He told me to tell you if you showed up, and if you still want to see him, he's at home with dinner waiting."

Hunter stared at Walker in silence. He wasn't sure he'd heard right. "Seriously? Trace doesn't cook."

A smile exploded across Walker's face. "I didn't say he cooked it."

Without any input from his brain, hope exploded in his chest. "Thanks for letting me know."

Walker's smile didn't abate. "Good luck, man. I'm rooting for you."

Hunter managed a small smile in return. Before that moment, he hadn't thought Walker cared much for him, which only mattered because Trace cared about Walker. No doubt his opinions influenced Trace's. With a final nod, Hunter made the trip back to his car. Some of his earlier exhaustion disappeared, buoyed by excitement. They'd be alone. For the first time since Hunter had ruined everything, he felt like he had a shot again. By the time he made it to Trace's cabin, that excitement had transformed into full blown terror. There was a real probability this was it. He'd learn tonight if they were over or not. This was his final shot. His knuckles barely connected with the door when it opened. Trace stood on the other side, looking every bit as scared.

A tug in Hunter's chest had him taking a breath. His eyes stung. He didn't want to lose this man. Hunter blinked, fighting the emotions overwhelming him. His mouth opened. Even Hunter didn't know what he intended to say. Everything hurt, and he was so tired. "I love you."

Trace visibly swallowed while Hunter tried to decide if that pained voice had really been his. "I love you too."

They stood in Trace's open doorway, staring at each other. Neither of them moved. It was as if they had a silent understanding. Hunter would either come inside and they'd work for each other from now on, or Hunter would leave now and never look back. "I never, ever wanted to hurt you. You just stormed into my life and I didn't know how to make space for you or be who you needed. I'm still learning, but I want to be wherever you are."

"It's not all on you," Trace said, surprising Hunter. "I fell really hard really fast, and I expected you to feel the same. You've had a lot going on for a really long time and I don't think I did enough to make sure you know you're the only one for me."

Hunter shook his head. "There's a selfish part of me that wants you to meet me halfway on the guilt, but I can't. Everything you said in that letter was true except for me using you. I never thought about your money at all, especially since you don't really live like you have as much as you do. You made it easy for me to forget you are so much better than I am. But you were right about everything else. I was embarrassed for people to know I was dating someone younger than my son. No one I know has ever seen me date a man." Trace winced, but Hunter kept talking because Trace deserved the truth. "I don't know how I expected to move past all that without trying, but maybe I also expected you'd get bored and move on or someone younger and better would sweep you away. You're right to be angry about all of that. You didn't deserve to be treated like you were a hot piece I made time for only when and where it was convenient for me. I didn't do anything to deserve you or your love. You shouldn't be seeing me now. The only thing I can do is try to prove every day from here on out that I'm not ashamed, I don't care what anyone thinks, and I do love you so fucking much that being without you is killing me. Nothing else matters to me anymore. Lane went in to rehab yesterday, but before he did, we had a long talk. I'm going to let the house go. We decided together that it's okay for me to admit I can't be the person who was married to his mother anymore and just move forward. I don't know where I'm headed from here, but I know I want to be with you no matter what else happens in my life."

Trace didn't respond and his expression kept his thoughts hidden. When the moment came that Hunter thought he might break down if Trace didn't put him out of his misery, Trace finally spoke. "You're letting all my heat out."

Despite the seriousness of the situation, a smile snapped to Hunter's lips.

Trace's expression never wavered. "Seriously, in or out. Make a decision. I'm not paying to heat the neighborhood."

A laugh sneaked out at Trace's old man voice. He shook his head. "In, if you'll still have me."

Trace stepped back, silently inviting Hunter inside. Hunter sucked in his sexy scent as he passed. His palms itched to touch Trace. His entire body ached with need. Instead of reaching for Trace, Hunter shoved his hands in his pockets. Too many times, Hunter had chosen to make love to Trace rather than show his love. He needed to do things differently than he did the first time around.

Hunter cleared his throat. Even to his ears, he sounded uncomfortable. "So Walker said you ordered dinner. Is it something you can put in the fridge so I can take you out instead?"

The sweetest smile Hunter had ever seen touched Trace's lips. "You've been out enough lately. Can we relax tonight?"

Hunter wondered if he should put up a fight. He wanted to stay in. God knew he was tired, but he'd rather drag his exhausted ass around for the rest of his life than live without Trace.

A sexy chuckle rumbled through the air. Trace's bright smile had the tightness in Hunter's chest easing. "Stop internally panicking. I'm being serious. Let's stay in. Not only do we need a night away from crowds, we should talk, don't you think?"

Hunter nodded. Damn, he didn't like feeling uncomfortable with Trace. They'd felt so indestructible before he'd fucked everything up with his stupid shit.

Trace's smile fell. "Okay. I'm sorry. I can't take it." Hunter lost his breath. He'd known Trace taking him back was too good to be true. Trace closed the distance between them, wrapped his arms around Hunter's waist, and held on. He pressed his cheek to Hunter's chest and squeezed. Hunter's shock quickly faded. His arms encircled Trace. The moment he held Trace, Hunter's throat swelled. The backs of eyes burned. He swallowed, trying to fight the wave of emotions.

"I love you." The words croaked from Hunter, sounding as painful as they were. "Please don't leave me again." He shook. The fear of never holding Trace again had been real.

Trace sniffed. Hunter nearly blacked out from the instant rage that washed over him. If anyone else on the planet made Trace cry, Hunter would smile as he gutted them. To know that it was him who'd caused this, he'd never been more ashamed. His hold tightened. He couldn't squeeze Trace hard enough to satisfy his need to fix things.

"Hunter."

"What is it, baby?"

"Do you want to talk about the erection between us?"

The question surprised a laugh from Hunter. He assessed his body. Yep, he was hard. Funny how he hadn't even noticed. It seemed his body knew it was being held by sexiest man alive while his brain had been dealing with every other emotion. Still, now wasn't the time.

"I don't know what you're talking about."

Trace's body shook with barely suppressed laughter. He swiped his face on his shoulder and tilted his chin up to meet Hunter's stare. His beautiful blue eyes were red rimmed, and the tip of his nose was red. Hunter swore he heard his heart shatter. "You're so beautiful. Why do you waste your time on me?"

Trace's mouth lifted in one corner. "Because I know you're trying to be the one, and that's so much more than anyone else has to offer."

Trace was right. Hunter was trying to be the one for Trace, and he would never stop. He would dog Trace's heels until his final breath, because—even though it hadn't looked like it in a while—they had something so fucking beautiful. "Is it okay if we just go to bed? I don't mean for sex," Hunter rushed to add. "I want to hold you and hold you some more."

Trace nodded. He took Hunter's hand and headed for the bedroom. At the edge of the bed, they stopped while Hunter toed off his shoes and Trace turned down the blankets. They exchanged glances while stripping to their underwear. Trace climbed onto the mattress. Hunter followed. He tugged Trace into his arms as they settled in.

Hunter meant to tuck the man against his chest. Instead, Trace took control and kissed him. Hunter's heart overflowed with love. He knew then they'd be okay, because he would never let anything touch them ever again.

If Trace had any doubts about taking Hunter back, they died away as Hunter drifted off to sleep in his arms. Hunter loved him. No one could see the way Hunter looked at him and have any doubts. Trace's heart was full.

For a long while, Trace kept his ear pressed to Hunter's chest, listening to his heart beat. He loved that sound. It was proof that the other half of his soul lived. When real life couldn't be avoided any longer, Trace quietly slipped from the bed. He moved in increments, ensuring he didn't wake Hunter as he went. Hunter was exhausted. The dark circles under Hunter's eyes hurt Trace's heart. Hunter needed sleep. Trace was used to staying up all night and there was food on his kitchen table, going bad. He quietly moved around the kitchen, boxing the food he'd set out earlier. He'd put it in the fridge for now and ask Hunter later if he thought it was still good. Trace wasn't good at adulting. He rarely ate at home, since he wasn't there often. Maybe one day, he'd learn to cook. A smile tugged at the corners of his mouth. Maybe Hunter would teach him, or they could take one of those cooking classes for couples. He stopped and looked at his kitchen. It was too small and there was none of things he'd seen in Hunter's kitchen. Trace's smile fell. Hunter planned to let his house go. He hadn't cashed Trace's check, which Trace had known, but still. Where would Hunter and Lane go? Lane was old enough to be on his own, but he wouldn't be ready for that the second he left rehab. Hunter could stay with Trace, but Trace didn't have room for the three of them in this tiny rental cabin.

Trace turned in a slow circle, trying to decide what to do. His gaze landed on the doorway, where Hunter stood leaned against the doorframe and watching him. He jumped in surprise. "Holy shit, baby." He patted his chest, trying to slow his racing heart. "I thought you were sleeping."

"I was, but my arms got lonely. Why did you run off?"

Trace motioned toward the fridge. "I had to put the food up before it went bad. Then I just sort of spaced out, thinking."

A line appeared between Hunter's eyebrows. "What's wrong?"

Trace's hands lifted before falling back to his sides. "I think I need a bigger place."

The smile that stretched Hunter's lips fascinated Trace. He looked entertained by Trace. "You're never here. Why do you need a bigger place?"

"For you and Lane."

Hunter's smile faltered. "You..." Hunter cleared his throat. "Are you..." Hunter visibly struggled to find his words. "Why?"

"You said you're letting the house go, and you won't accept my money. You'll need a place to go. This place is just a rental, and it's too small for everyone. How do you feel about that subdivision about a block from Incubus? You know, that one on the right before you go over that huge hill? Those houses look nice and the neighborhood looks quiet. It's a gated community, I think?" Hunter wasn't saying anything, but he was smiling. Trace's eyebrows rose. "What?"

Hunter shook his head. His smile grew. "I'm just wrapping my head around you. Is this how everything will be with us? Will I wake up married one day or will you let me ask?"

Trace realized he was doing it again, storming into Hunter's life and taking over. But Hunter was smiling. Trace chewed his bottom lip. He felt like shit. "Sorry."

Hunter's smile fell. He pushed away from the doorframe and crossed the room. "Don't apologize. I love it," Hunter said, tugging Trace into his arms. "I never have to worry about where I stand with you. It's freeing. Wherever you want to live, that's what we'll do. As long as we're together, I don't care."

A self-deprecating smile pulled at Trace's lips. "You say that now, but you haven't seen how far I can go when I'm on a roll. I'll take over your whole life. You need to call me on things when I get carried away. I don't know why I'm this way." Maybe he was the obsessive one who needed to see all his ideas come to life, not Lane. Perhaps he was the one he should be psychoanalyzing.

"You have too much confidence," Hunter said, not sparing his feelings, but his voice was filled with love. "I love everything about you, even that. You're also a little kinky," Hunter added with a sexy chuckle. "It's a deadly combo."

Trace took a breath, trying to reel in his over-the-top happiness. He pulled Hunter's scent in with the air. Hunter smelled like home. Trace burrowed his face in Hunter's hold and inhaled again. His cock stirred. Trace ignored it. "I want to ask what your plans were before I took over and started planning your future, but I'm scared your plans didn't really include me."

"My plans always include you." Hunter's voice rumbled against Trace's ear, making him smile. "Now that that's out of the way, do you want to talk about the erection between us?"

Trace bit his lip, holding back the happiness. "I don't know. Do you? You're so tired. I can practically feel it."

"I'm never too tired for you."

Trace's fingertips skimmed down Hunter's body, heading toward what he wanted. "I don't know. I can be pretty exhausting."

A sexy flush appeared on Hunter's cheeks, fascinating Trace. "You feed my soul."

A lump formed in Trace's throat. It sounded in his voice. "I've missed you so much. It's been a hole in my gut. I'm empty without you." He curled his fingers around the waistband of Hunter's underwear. "You should make it better." He took a step forward, backing Hunter against the counter. Trace held Hunter's stare as he pushed the underwear down his hips. He kneeled and helped Hunter completely out of his clothes. With Hunter nude, Trace slowly came back to his feet, pausing midway to drag his tongue up Hunter's length. Hunter hissed and clung to the edge of the counter. Trace smirked. They were just getting started.

"Don't move," Trace warned. He moved to the nearest cabinet and found a jar of coconut oil. "Are you allergic to this?" Trace held the jar up for Hunter.

Hunter shook his head.

Trace set the jar aside and stripped. The way Hunter watched him had Trace throbbing. He had patience and a plan. Trace could feel Hunter's heated gaze upon him as he moved around the kitchen. Hunter was smart, though. He didn't move as Trace ordered. First, Trace moved a dining room chair to Hunter's side.

He pointed at the rungs at the bottom. "One foot there."

Even though Hunter looked confused, he dutifully set his foot on the rung.

Trace winked and grabbed a second chair, positioning it in front of Hunter.

He retrieved the oil. Hunter never looked away as Trace scooped out a handful of white goop, rubbing his hands together and turning it to oil. Trace started at Hunter's hips and worked inward. Hunter's skin glistened with oil. By the time Trace made it to Hunter's cock, Hunter was audibly panting. Trace didn't stop with his dick. He moved lower, rubbing the oil on Hunter's balls before moving to his asshole. Trace teased without mercy, massaging the spot between Hunter's balls and hole. Hunter's lips were slightly parted. His eyes looked unfocused. A sexy flush rode his cheeks.

He used a ton of oil, ensuring Hunter's comfort as he eased one finger inside. Hunter's breath left in a loud whoosh. His knuckles whitened as he tightened his grip on the counter. Trace hid a smile. He mimicked the motions of sex as he worked a second finger inside. A soft whimper escaped Hunter as Trace found the spongy spot inside Hunter that would drive him insane. He rubbed. Hunter's eyes fell closed on a moan. Trace's dick tapped his stomach, reminding Trace it was being ignored. He tugged Hunter's cock instead, watching as Hunter's crown disappeared inside his fist even as continued massaging Hunter internally with his other hand.

Trace leaned in and kissed Hunter's stomach. "Do you remember when you said I could fuck you?"

Hunter whimpered in response.

Trace took it as a yes. "It's about to happen," Trace promised. "But first, you need to relax."

Hunter dropped his chin and stared at Trace with so much heat that pre-cum rolled down Trace's length. Hunter's hips rolled, as if he couldn't stop it from happening. "I need to make room for my cock," Trace whispered, hoping not to spook Hunter as he pushed a third finger inside Hunter's ass. The sexiest sound Trace had ever heard left Hunter's lips. Trace kept him there, drawing him closer to the edge. He coated his own erection with oil, using way more than necessary. "You're going to straddle this chair and sit on my dick now. I promise I'll make you feel good."

Hunter shifted positions. He watched Trace with so much trust, Trace's chest felt tight with pride.

"You can do this," Trace whispered as Hunter straddled him. "We'll go slow." He swiped Hunter's asshole with his crown before easing inside a hair. Hunter hissed. Trace jacked Hunter's cock, distracting him. Hunter bit his bottom lip as he settled onto Trace's dick. Trace praised him the whole way. "That's it, baby. You have no idea how brave you are. We're going slow. You don't have to move. I wish you knew how good you feel. You're so hot on my cock." Hunter rocked forward and Trace held him still. "It's okay. You're adjusting to me. Just stay put. You can make me fly like this. I promise. Lean back a little, sexy. I want you to find that spot that feels good and stay put."

While holding on to the back of the chair, Hunter tilted his hips. A moan vibrated through him as Trace's cock hit just the right spot. "Goddamn, Trace."

Trace massaged Hunter's dick. "Good boy. Don't move. Just feel." Trace was so close to blowing, but he needed Hunter to enjoy this or he might not ever do it again. They had a lot of years left together. Trace wanted them to be as adventurous as possible. He needed Hunter to have something with him he hadn't experienced anywhere else. Trace needed to be special. He pumped Hunter's cock, handling it as if it was his own. He moved from root to crown, squeezing lightly each time he reached the tip. He kept his pace steady. Hunter's body kept trying to tug Trace deeper. It was getting harder by the second to ignore the pressure climbing his shaft. Hunter threw his head back, straining against Trace's hand. Trace increased his pace. He needed Hunter's orgasm. Hunter's body hardened. Trace gasped as Hunter's already too tight asshole clamped tighter. Hot cum hit Trace's chest. A loud cry filled the air. Trace no longer knew who it belonged to. Hunter's ass squeezed and sucked at Trace's cock. An orgasm slammed into Trace, stealing his breath. He couldn't stop massaging Hunter's dick—like he was tugging out his own pleasure. Trace gasped and fought for air. Open mouthed, he sucked air, trying to get oxygen to his brain. Hunter was so goddamn mind-blowing. Trace couldn't wait to spend the rest of his life with this man.

He gently pushed Hunter away, just enough to ease from inside him, before pulling him closer and capturing Hunter's mouth. Hunter sounded winded, but he didn't stop kissing Trace to catch his breath. They licked each other's tongues, twining and retreating. Both of them fought to get closer. Kiss deeper. Trace couldn't stop massaging every place he could reach. Love bled from his every pore. He'd never felt closer to anyone. Trace didn't know how to vocalize it, so he kept touching Hunter, trying to make him feel it.

"I love you, sexy," Trace said between kisses.

Hunter pulled away just enough to press his forehead to Trace's. "I love you too. So much."

Trace kept rubbing Hunter every place he could reach. He couldn't stop touching him. "Did I hurt you?"

Hunter shook his head. "I want to spend the rest of my life with you. The only way you could hurt me is to leave again. I just want this."

"I'm not going anywhere," Trace promised. "I've already got a million ideas on how to spend our time. You don't want to miss the life I'm already planning for you."

A tired sounding laugh escaped Hunter. "I can't wait."

Trace couldn't stop smiling. He knew he was a lot to handle. It hadn't escaped his notice he was a tad obsessive and didn't stop until he had everything he wanted. It was a good thing Hunter loved him because Trace had been one hundred percent real. He had plans brewing. Some of them were naughty, but mostly, he had a beautiful life mapped out for Hunter. Trace would take care of him. Hunter never had to stress ever again. As long as they worked to hang on, they couldn't possibly fail. It was love.

Chapter Nine

IT HAD BEEN THREE months since Lane entered rehab and it was the first day they'd been allowed to visit. Hunter hadn't realized how much he would miss his son while he was gone. He tapped his foot, incapable of holding back his nervous energy while waiting for Lane to join them in the garden area. The center where Lane was staying was fucking amazing. It was nicer than most resorts. Trace hadn't admitted he'd been the one to make the arrangements for Lane until two weeks after they'd moved in together. It had been a smart move on Trace's part, because Hunter hadn't been happy. His biggest fear, except for losing Trace, was Trace thinking Hunter wanted his money. That would probably always be an issue since he'd already lost Trace once over it. Hunter had only stayed mad about an hour. Then, Trace kissed him and charmed him, painting a picture of a future where Lane was healthy. It had broken his heart to learn the reason behind his son's addiction. Lacy and he had spent so many years focused on her rapidly deteriorating health, Lane had shifted to the back burner when no one had been watching. Some days, Hunter wondered why Trace wanted him at all. He obviously wasn't very good at taking care of the people he loved. Hunter was working on it, though. Maybe he wasn't perfect, but he loved Trace and Lane. He wouldn't fail them again.

A soft chuckle caressed Hunter's ears, making him smile. Trace pushed down on Hunter's knee, trying to hold it still. "Stop, baby. There's no reason to be so nervous."

He glanced over while chewing the side of his nail. Trace shook his head and pried Hunter's hand from his mouth, making him realize what he'd been do-ing. He flashed Trace a smile that felt pained. Hunter couldn't imagine how it looked. "What if, now that Lane's clean, he realizes I've been a shit father?"

"You're not."

Hunter wasn't appeased. "But what if he does?"

Trace looked damn near saint-like as he took a breath. His gaze never wavered from Hunter. "You're not a shit father. Think about this, what if Lane's nervous because he's clean now and wonders if you've realized he's a shit son?"

"But he's not," Hunter argued without missing a beat.

Trace nodded. "Exactly. Neither of you are shit. Everyone struggles with something, but you love each other. You're there for each other. Nothing has changed. You'll see."

He sounded so confident, Hunter couldn't help but believe. That belief disappeared as quickly as it manifested. Lane stepped outside. His hair was shaggy, and he'd gained a little weight. He was still skinny as hell, but his face didn't look as sharply edged. He smiled as he headed in their direction. Hunter shot to his feet. A lump rose in his throat. His eyes burned as he wrapped his arms around his son.

"Hey, Dad," Lane said against his chest.

Even Hunter's breath shook. "Hey, son." He leaned away and eyed the face of the boy he'd raised. His green eyes were clear for the first time in forever. Hunter couldn't stop staring at him. "You look good."

Lane's flashed him a crooked smile. "You too. Marriage agrees with you." It did. Hunter couldn't argue with that. Even though he'd only convinced Trace to marry him three days ago, he knew how that quick exchanging of vows showed on his face. He was so fucking proud and ecstatic. Without those rings and paper, he'd felt oddly on edge—like Trace would wake up any second and realize he didn't want Hunter. Hearing Trace repeat his vows had been one of the greatest moments of Hunter's life. He'd never let Trace regret him. They'd told Lane over the phone, but Hunter had worried he'd only pretended to be happy for them, considering Trace was younger than Lane. The way Lane smiled now made Hunter realize he'd worried over nothing.

Lane moved to Trace's side. "Look at you. You look so happy," he said, hugging Trace. "Should I call you Dad too now?"

Trace rolled his eyes. "Please don't."

Hunter couldn't stop smiling. His little family wasn't home together under the same roof yet, but they would be soon, which reminded Hunter.

"We got all your stuff moved to the new house."

"The place is smaller," Trace warned, chiming in. "But your room is bigger."

Hunter rolled his eyes at the warning. He'd been forced to stop Trace from buying a huge place. Trace made it hard as hell for Hunter to prove he didn't want Trace's money. Trace kept trying to spend it. Not to mention, they had other things going on and wouldn't be at home as much.

Lane waved off Trace's claim. "I'm not worried over it. I'm just glad you're still giving me a place to live when I leave here, until I can figure things out."

Trace sat back down at the picnic table and Lane joined him. Hunter moved at a slower pace. He was too busy enjoying seeing his boys together.

Trace waved for him to hurry. "Don't even think about it. We want you there. Plus, we kind of had an idea we wanted to run by you. If you're up to hearing it right now?"

Hunter filled the spot beside Trace and held his hand beneath the table.

Lane looked between them expectantly. "Go for it. I'm good."

He was. Hunter could see how far he'd come. Trace glanced his way as if waiting for him to start. Hunter cleared his throat. "Well, I've been miserable at Gray Steel Designs for a long time now and Trace didn't really plan to stay here in Colorado forever. I'm tired of working my ass off and other people making the money and taking the credit. He's got the golden business touch. So Trace put Walker in charge of Incubus, and we plan to travel around and start new hot spots in different towns that Trace has pinpointed as ready to explode with nightlife activity. I'm going to do the building designs and help out with whatever else he needs, and he's going to put them on the map."

"That's awesome," Lane said, sounding truly thrilled.

"We were hoping," Trace said, cutting in, "that you would hold our fort down while we're gone on jobs and help Walker out around the club with the books and whatnot. You don't really need to be serving drinks while trying to stay sober. In exchange, if you're still feeling like it's something you want and can handle, I will fund your dispensary like promised, but you won't have to pay me back, and I won't take any profits. It'll be one hundred percent yours."

Lane's smile faltered. "Are you sure you trust me to do all that? That's a lot, considering..."

"You won't let us down." Trace sounded so sure. Hunter couldn't look away from his confidence. Trace was amazing. Hunter had never felt luckier. If Trace hadn't burst into his life, everything would be a mess. Lane might've been dead by now. Hunter's throat swelled at the thought. He rubbed his thumb against Trace's in his rising panic. Sometimes he had to remind himself this was real.

Lane cleared his throat. "If you're sure that's what you want, I'd love to try."

Hunter tore his gaze away from Trace and focused on Lane. He was so damn proud of his son. It took a lot of courage to admit he didn't know if he'd be okay. Trying was all Hunter needed. Lane trying was more than he'd ever expected.

"We're sure," Hunter said, letting Lane know they were together on this.

Lane looked between them. "I love you guys. I've missed you. Walker has been telling me how great you are together, but I'm so happy to see it for myself."

"We love you too. When did you talk to Walker?"

Lane looked uncomfortable for the first time since they arrived. He glanced away. "We talk almost every day. He's helping me with some stuff. He's a good person." There was something in Lane's voice. Hunter didn't dig. If Walker helped in some way, Hunter was grateful.

"So tell us everything," Trace said, keeping the conversation moving. "This place is very resort-like. How is everything going?"

Lane fell into telling them about his stay while Hunter's gaze moved between Trace and him. Hope slapped Hunter in the face. For the first time, Hunter realized how bright the future looked. Until that moment, he hadn't realized how much Trace had transformed his outlook. After quitting his job and letting the house go, a lot had changed between them. Hunter wasn't tired all the time and they were always together. Now he found it funny when someone younger hit on Trace when they were at Incubus, because Hunter knew Trace was his. No one could take him away. He squeezed Trace's hand because he couldn't stop. This sometimes cocky, extremely confident, deliciously kinky man had saved him. Trace was still too young and too good for Hunter, but Hunter gave no fucks now. As long as Trace wanted him, Hunter would see that love and desire for the blessing it was. For as long as he lived, Hunter intended to deserve Trace. His every action would be an attempt to earn this beautiful bulldozer who'd swept him away. Hunter didn't care what anyone thought about them. He never looked away from Trace long enough to see their opinions anyhow. This was their heaven, their story, and it was perfect.

Keep an eye out for the next book in the Sugar Babies series, *Broken Baby*.

Please consider leaving a review at the retailer where this book was purchased. Reviews really help with a book's visibility, which ensures I can continue writing. Thank you, Charity.

About the Author

About the Author

Charity Parkerson is an award-winning and multi-published author with several companies. Born with no filter from her
brain to her mouth, she decided to take this odd quirk and insert it in her characters.

*Eight-time Readers' Favorite Award Winner

CHARITY PARKERSON

*2015 Passionate Plume Award Finalist
*2013 Reviewers' Choice Award Winner
*2012 ARRA Finalist for Favorite Para-
normal
Romance
*Five-time winner of The Mistress of
the
Darkpath

Connect with her online:

*Sign up for her newsletter: https://sen
dfox.com/charityparkerson
*Join her readers' group on Facebook:
http://bit.ly/CharitysTribe
*Website: https://www.charityparkerso
n.com
*A list of her social media accounts and
giveaways all in one place: http://hy.pa
ge/charityparkerson